POTLUCK AND PANDEMONIUM

S.C. MERRITT

S.C. MERRITT

To Momma who encourages me to follow my dreams.

CONTENTS

ACKNOWLEDGMENTS

I want to thank everyone who has encouraged me to take the leap to write about what I enjoy . . . and that is murder.

A million thanks to all my friends who have read and given me valuable feedback and suggestions.

Especially my friend and fellow author Kelly A. Walker, who has walked me through this process and helped me with everything from website design to editing. Your help has been invaluable.

Thanks to Linda Rettstatt. You have encouraged me and I doubt that I would've come this far if I hadn't found our little group.

Special thanks to my Mom who encourages me endlessly and convinces me that I can do anything and for the brainstorming sessions about all the ways to commit murder.

To my son, who advises on all things graphic design and computer related since I am so tech-challenged.

To my daughter, for all the beta reading, suggestions and recipes.

And, to my awesome husband, who lets me chase my dreams and doesn't complain (too much) when I spend money in the process.

PROLOGUE

I jerked the steering wheel to the left as that irritating grinding noise roused my wandering mind back to reality. I guided my Honda off the grids on the shoulder of the interstate back into the lane and tried to clear my mind. It was beginning to rain again, so I clicked my wipers into high gear and glanced in my rearview mirror to make sure I was still being followed. My brother, Jake, who had generously used a couple of his vacation days at work to come to Texas and help load and move me back to Alabama, was currently behind me in a rental truck. It hadn't been an easy decision for me, but it was definitely the right one.

Thirty years ago last September, my husband and I entered into married bliss and promptly moved to Buckhead, Texas, a very small suburb north of Dallas. Eighteen months ago, I became a widow. We loved our little town, but after Dave's death, I was thrown for a loop. I wasn't sure about anything anymore. I had always been a bit of a worrier. You know, one of those crazy people who drives down the road and imagines scenarios like: what I should do when I top the next hill and someone is heading toward me in my lane? What does the ditch look like on my right? Is there a tree I need to avoid? Could I keep the car from flipping if I ran up that embankment up ahead? Well, without Dave there, it really started getting out of hand. Every time the phone rang, I would imagine bad news. After awhile I had to make a decision. I knew it was time for a fresh start and I needed to get back home.

Dave was an accountant. Just a regular, hard-working, certified public accountant. He got his degree from the University of Alabama, just like me. Except my degree, is in Interior Design. We were in love and had big dreams. He took a job right out of college with a small firm in Dallas named Johnson & Fredrickson. He had offers from larger firms but he decided to go with a smaller one so he could spend more time at home when we decided to start a family. As it turned out, that took about a minute since I ended up getting pregnant on our honeymoon.

Nine months later, our daughter, Macy, was born and I stayed home with her until she skipped off to Kindergarten. Dave was still plugging away at debits and credits when I decided to see if I could remember anything I learned in college and started working part time as a designer with a local interior design firm. Dave worked a few late nights every month, just like most accountants do when he had to close out the books from the month before and periodically, he would have to travel to meet with clients who weren't local. We loved every minute of our lives together. We had great friends and a great life. Everything was perfect. The years passed and Macy grew up and went off to college and just like that, we were empty-nesters. Dave gradually started traveling more so I started working more hours to fill the time.

One night, when Dave was working late at the office, there was a knock at the door. I dragged myself out of my comfy recliner where I was enthralled in a rerun of Murder, She Wrote, placed my Diet Coke on the side table and shuffled to the door. I peeked through the glass and fear immediately rose in my throat. I didn't recognize either of the men standing on the porch, but I had a feeling it was bad news. I inched the door open.

"Can I help you?"

"Mrs. Glory Harper?" One of them asked.

"Yes."

"My name is Officer Grady Bonner with the Buckhead Police Department. May we come in?"

I backed away from the door and let them step inside.

"Mrs. Harper, I'm sorry to have to tell you, but your husband, David Harper, has been killed."

I sucked in a breath and felt myself about to faint as my knees buckled. One of the men caught me and eased me over to a chair to sit down. This couldn't be happening.

"What happened? Was it a car accident?"

"No ma'am. I'm afraid his body was found in a parking garage. In Reno, Nevada."

"What? That's not possible! He works in Dallas. He would have told me if he was traveling for work today. I'm sure you must have the wrong person."

But he didn't. I asked them more questions, but either they didn't know the answers, or they weren't allowed to tell me. Looking back now, I'm pretty sure it was the latter.

The next weeks and months were a blur. After the funeral, it took me months before I could even open the door to Dave's home office. The men from his firm had come immediately to pick up his work laptop and any client files he had brought home, so the rest of it sat just as he left it.

The one thing I did do was stay in touch with the police about the investigation. If they didn't call me at least every other day, I called them. Detective John Bridgestone was the man in charge of the case.

"Detective Bridgestone, this is Glory Harper again. Do you have any new leads on Dave's case?"

"Hello, Mrs. Harper. No, we are still trying to piece together what little bit of evidence we have. You know that the security cameras in the parking garage had been disabled and there were no other witnesses, so it's going to be a slow process."

"What about fingerprints? Did you check his body or his car for those? Maybe the killer touched him. What about fibers? Were there any pieces of clothing or fibers off fabric that your men found?"

"No ma'am. Since it was on an outdoor level of the garage, the wind would've carried any of that type of evidence away immediately." I could hear him blow out a long, irritated breath.

"His wallet was empty except for his driver's license, so we are pretty sure it was a random mugging, Mrs. Harper."

"What about the fact that he was in Reno, Nevada, and

he never even mentioned to me that he was going out of town when he left that morning. Surely that must have something to do with it."

"I don't want to speak ill of the dead, Mrs. Harper, but I think maybe you need to reconcile yourself to the possibility that he may have been in Reno to see another woman. That's why he didn't tell you he was going out of town."

I disconnected the call and sat down on the edge of the bed. The phone dropped to the floor at my feet as I just stared into space, numb to everything. I knew deep in my heart that Dave was not unfaithful to me. Our love was strong and enduring. Built on faith and trust. He would never do that to me. I know he was a man who wasn't perfect. It can happen to anyone, but if there was nothing else in this world that I knew for sure, I knew that Dave Harper loved me.

After about six months of having essentially the same conversation every week, the phone rang. When I saw Detective Bridgestone's name scroll across the screen, my heart raced. *He never calls me. I am always the one to call him. They must have a break in the case! Something that will finally give us some closure and find justice for Dave.*

"Hello, Detective Bridgestone." I answered, trying to steady my breathing.

"Mrs. Harper," he said matter-of-factly.

"Do you have good news? Do you have new leads?"

"I know this is not what you have hoped to hear, Mrs. Harper, but we have made the decision to declare it a cold case and shelve it indefinitely."

My heart sank. After all these months, he finally said

the words I was dreading. I knew it was coming sooner or later.

"And Mrs. Harper – I know you are not happy that we have stopped the investigation, but I hope you will let this go. I would advise you to move on and above all, do not continue asking questions on your own. I really can't say more than this, but it wouldn't be safe. I'd hate for anything to happen to you."

"What do you mean... not safe? I thought you said this was a random robbery gone wrong? Surely you don't think some thug robber from Reno, Nevada, is going to come looking for me all the way to Dallas, Texas. Is there something you aren't telling me, Detective?"

"I've already said too much, Mrs. Harper. Just leave it alone or I'm afraid you'll regret it." The phone line went dead.

I got up and walked down the hall to Dave's office. I grasped the doorknob, took a deep breath and turned it. The air in the room smelled a little stale after months of being closed off, but I could have sworn I could still smell Dave's cologne. Macy had given him a bottle of his favorite last Christmas.

I sat down at his desk and opened drawer after drawer. I thought it was odd that the detective had never asked to go through Dave's office. They never once asked to see any of his files. I knew there had to be something in here that could give me some kind of clue about why he was in Reno. I searched for an hour and all I found were files related to our personal finances. Paid bills files, copies of Macy's college payments, binders full of instructions and owner's manuals for every appliance in the house. But nothing related to his work. Where was his briefcase? I'm sure he had it with him, but it was never found. How odd that they would take everything except his driver's license. A mugger would have taken the whole wallet and not take the time to just remove the cash. And a robber also wouldn't have thought to wear gloves so they wouldn't leave fingerprints on the wallet. None of it made sense, yet the police had just given up. The more I thought about it, the more I was convinced that someone put pressure on them to shut down the investigation. But who? And why?

The next morning, I brought in several boxes I had saved from grocery deliveries and began boxing up everything in Dave's desk and labeling carefully. I had just pulled out the last file from the bottom left drawer when I accidentally knocked a pen off the desk into the drawer. The sound it made caught my attention. It was a hollow sound, not like a solid oak drawer at all. I reached into the drawer and tapped on the bottom. The base of the drawer shifted away from the wall of the drawer. I used the pen to pry up a false bottom. Hidden underneath was something that would change my life forever.

There in the bottom of the drawer were four large brown envelopes. I spread them out on the desktop. The first envelope I opened contained several US Passports with Dave's picture, but different names. I opened the passports one by one.

Steven Goldsmith from Wyoming.

Matthew Green from New York.

William Brotherton from Kansas.

The last one flipped open and it wasn't a passport. It

was an ID badge for Special Agent, David Harper for the FBI.

I sat there stunned. Like I was living in a nightmare and couldn't wake up. Was this real? Was my husband a secret agent for the US government and I didn't know it? How long had this been going on? How long had he been lying to me? I looked at the issue date of the ID card. 2009. Ten years? He'd been lying to me for ten years? And what on earth did the FBI need an accountant for?

I picked up one of the other envelopes. Written on the front was the name Salvatore "Big Sal" Cardinelli. I opened it up and found copies of what looked like ledger pages and computer printouts of bank records along with a computer flash drive. Pictures of a short, squatty little man with a cigar in his mouth walking out of a restaurant in some big city. Maybe New York City?

The writing on the second envelope said Frank "The Fixer" Fishetti. It held the same type of papers, another flash drive and snapshots, but these were of a paunchy, middle-aged man with a greasy black mustache. He had on a dark suit, a fedora balanced on his bald head and a blonde bombshell on each arm. They looked to be in Vegas, maybe. The women had on showgirl costumes with beads dangling from any place that had enough fabric to sew a bead on to.

I flipped over the last envelope and stopped. The name written on it was Glory. I pinched open the clasp on the last envelope and inside was a stack of money. I slowly pulled out the stack banded together with a paper band. Ten thousand dollars in one-hundred-dollar bills. It was clear now, that he must have been helping investigate illegal accounting practices like money laundering and embezzlement. There was no mistaking the names on the envelopes were connected to organized crime. I held the envelope upside down and tapped it. A white piece of paper folded in half floated out onto the desktop. I picked it up and opened it.

My Glory Bug, if you're reading this, it must be because I'm gone. I'm sorry for all this has probably put you through but I want you to know one thing, I have loved you forever and forever I will.

I know how much you love your TV sleuths, but please don't try to dig any further into this. It's much too dangerous. Hold on to these envelopes and keep them safe. If you ever find someone that you would trust with your life, maybe this information will help bring justice. Use this cash (don't worry, it's clean money) along with the insurance money to start over. Maybe back in Alabama. It's home. Kiss my Macy for me. I'll see you again someday. Love, Dave.

I almost laughed as I wiped away the tears rolling down my cheeks. Dave knew me better than anyone and he knew how much I love a mystery. He knew I would be torn between wanting—no, needing to find justice and closure for us and needing to move on like he wanted me to. It's not just Dave's case, though. Something deep in me hates to see crimes go unpunished. I have to admit it's still a daily struggle to consciously put the past behind me and live in the present, looking forward to the future. But I was willing to give it my best shot.

The rain had slacked up again and I was getting

hungry. I hoped Jake would want to stop somewhere in Mississippi for a nice, greasy burger and fries. I reached over and adjusted the satellite radio station to Seriously Sinatra. As Frank belted out Fly Me to the Moon, I smiled. A new life was ahead. Dave wanted it and I needed it.

Alabama, I'm coming home.

CHAPTER 1

"Oh no, I think we should have left the house earlier. We may not get a parking space," my daughter, Macy, said looking at the sea of cars parked around the church as she turned into the parking lot.

"You can probably find a spot over there on the far side of the graveyard", I directed, pointing as we both gawked at the floral explosion outside. Worshipping the dead. That's what my Granny always called it, but it was known in the south as First Sunday in May, or Decoration Day, and it was a big, big deal. For most small country churches in Alabama, the first Sunday in May is the biggest weekend of the year with lots of family reunions and graveyard cleanups on Saturday. In a lot of small communities, the tradition has continued and grown to enormous, if not outlandish, proportions in some cases. By Sunday, it usually looked like the botanical gardens exploded outside the church. It's all capped off by the highlight of the weekend which is a special church service, followed by all-day singing and dinner on the ground. Over the years, dinner on the ground had become more of lunch on picnic tables, but it's always the site of massive amounts of the best home cooking you will find anywhere. My mouth watered just thinking about all the good desserts we would have to choose from spread out along the endless rows of tables under the shade of the huge trees in just a few hours. I had always had a tendency to carry a few extra pounds so I tried to be careful not to go crazy at these events, but I decided that I'd worry about that next week. A couple of extra laps around the neighborhood with my pup, Izzy, should take care of it. At least that's what I hoped. In the words of a true southern belle, Miss Scarlett O'Hara, "after all, tomorrow is another day", right?

There were quite a few more arrangements scattered around the graveyard than when we finished the cleanup at our family gravesite yesterday. I smoothed down the front of my new coral dress and checked for lipstick on my teeth in the mirror on the car's flip down sun visor.

"Mom, I'll let you out here so you won't have to traipse through the graveyard in your heels," Macy offered.

"Thanks, Sweetheart! I'll drop our food for the potluck off in the fellowship hall and meet you in the sanctuary."

Pausing in the doorway to the sanctuary, I glanced across the congregation and saw Momma's head craning around trying to find us. She spotted me and waved me over. I weaved my way around all the people who had been visiting in the aisle and were now scurrying to find a seat with their family members.

"Do you know how many people I had to knock off of this pew to save these seats for you?"

I laughed. "Momma, you're not serious!"

"No, but I had to tell a little white lie that you were gone to the ladies' room. It's a wonder I didn't get struck by lightning for lying in the Lord's House."

I watched as the choir filed into the choir loft. My sister in law, Kelly, sat on the front row with Linda Jenkins next to her on the end of the row. On a regular Sunday, the choir usually wore robes, but on special days like today and maybe Easter, the choir voted to go robe-less. Most of the ladies had new dresses and it seemed like such a waste to cover them up. I noticed Linda didn't have a new one. I had seen her wear that pretty floral print many times. Kelly mentioned to me once that Linda said her husband, J.R. didn't see the need for a new dress. In his opinion, they were a waste of money because "you don't get your money's worth out of a fancy Sunday dress." I glanced around and didn't see my brother, Jake, anywhere and then I remembered he said he was on duty at the police station this morning. Jake was a detective for the Sweetwater Springs Police Department. Macy squeezed in beside me and Momma just as we were all instructed to stand for the first hymn. *What a Friend We Have in Jesus.* One of Momma's favorites.

Kelly waggled her fingers in a little wave and smiled from the choir loft. I waved back and immediately noticed Linda's eyes grow wide. I watched as a panicked look came over her face when she looked toward my right. Following her gaze, I noticed J.R. standing two rows in front of us, on the other end of the pew. Next to him was a man I didn't recognize.

It was a very nice service. The choir did a bang-up job on the special songs they had been practicing. Just as Pastor Dan was closing out his sermon, I noticed the man next to J.R. slip out the side door toward the restrooms. The offertory music began and J.R. stood to help pass the offering plate. As head usher, he was in charge of taking the donations, placing them in the bank bag and dropping it in the secure locked drawer in the counting room back in the church office after the offering was taken.

As the pianist played a rollicking arrangement of *When We All Get to Heaven* for the offertory, her wig bobbing back and forth to the music, I leaned over to tell Macy that Momma and I had agreed to help Martha Jean Wilson set up the food on the picnic tables. We slipped out the back to make sure everything was ready for the rush that was about to come when the "amen" was said.

Martha Jean had an order to everything. That's why she was always put in charge of these things.

"I'm surprised Martha Jean isn't passing out table maps of where each type of food is supposed to go," I whispered to Momma. "Heaven forbid that a dish of green bean casserole should end up mixed in with the lemon lime congealed salads."

Momma giggled. "Where should we put our purses and Bibles? I would hate for them to get trampled or get something spilled on them."

"Let me have yours and I'll take them to the car. They should be safe from dirt and potato salad in there. Macy had to park on the other side of the graveyard, but it will only take me a couple minutes to walk them out there."

I gathered up our Bibles and purses and carefully picked my way through the graveyard, sidestepping to keep from stepping on graves. As I was ogling all the enormous flower arrangements throughout the gravesites, I stopped in my tracks. *"What is that over there? Is that a shoe poking out from behind that tree?"* I thought. "Hey, kids!" I called. "You don't need to be out here playing hide and seek around these graves. It's not safe, not to mention it's disrespectful." I waited for a response or a giggle, but the shoe didn't move. Just silence. "Hey! Did you hear me?" I raised my voice a little louder as I moved closer and rounded the tree prepared to grab a mischievous little boy by the sleeve. But it was no mischievous boy. It was a man. His glazed over cold eyes told me that he wasn't moving anytime soon. J.R. Jenkins was dead.

I screamed for anyone who was within earshot. "Help!! Somebody come out here quick!!" Momma came running around the side of the church. "Momma, get somebody, quick! Call Jake! I think J.R Jenkins is dead!"

I looked down at J.R. He was sitting there, pretty as you please, leaning up against a big tree in the middle of the graveyard. Except for the fact that his white dress shirt and blue tie were covered in blood, you could have put a glass of sweet tea in his hand and you would've thought he was sitting in the shade and enjoying the day. Lying next to the body was something I recognized immediately. It was a letter opener. *My* letter opener. The one I kept on my desk in the church office. It had my

initials engraved on the handle. It had been a gift from
Pastor Dan when I started the job at the church a few
months back.

I stared at J.R.'s chest, waiting to see the rise and fall of
breathing, but I was pretty sure there was none. I probably could have tried to find a pulse, but my hands were
shaking so much and I didn't think I should disturb the
body.

I heard the music stop inside the church, which meant
that the service was probably over. Any minute people
would come pouring out of the doors on the other side of
the church to be first in line at the picnic tables.

My heart was racing and I felt like I was going to be
sick as I tried not to look down at J.R.'s body. Finally,
Momma burst out the back door of the church followed
by Joe Bryan, who was on the church security team.

"Glory, honey, are you alright? What happened?"

"I don't know. He was just . . . there . . . " I stuttered,
pointing down at the body.

Momma stopped in her tracks, staring down wide-
eyed at the gruesome sight in front of us.

She wrapped her arms around my shoulders to try to
stop both of us from shaking.

"Why don't you just go sit down and take it easy until
Jake gets here." Momma instructed as Joe called 911.

"No, I'm fine," I confirmed. Even as my head was still
spinning, I felt a responsibility to help as much as I could.

The security team recruited several church members
and posted them in sort of a semicircle to serve as a
barrier trying to keep the people back from the scene
until the police got there. It was like herding cats, but

Pastor Dan was finally able to convince everyone to go back inside the church and wait until the police said it was okay for them to gather their belongings and leave.

"Make sure you don't let anybody touch anything!" I yelled. "This is a crime scene." I had seen enough mystery shows to know not to touch the letter opener. "Don't let anyone go near my office either!"

"What's your office got to do with anything?" Momma asked.

"Because it's probably what they call a secondary crime scene." I pointed at the letter opener. "If that turns out to be the murder weapon, then the killer had to have been in my office."

Momma looked at me like I was crazy, grabbing my arm and pulling me over to the side. "You sound like Jessica Fletcher! Don't you think you should just let Jake handle all this? It's not another one of our mystery shows. This is the real thing."

"Momma, this man was killed with *MY* letter opener, probably from *MY* office!" I whispered. "I'm just gonna keep my eyes and ears open for any clues I can pass on to Jake."

Several of the Sunday School ladies had gathered around Linda Jenkins over next to the back entrance to the church. Someone had pulled out a few folding chairs for them and they were comforting her as best they could. I walked over to them, offering my sympathy.

"Linda, I just don't know what to say. I'm so sorry about J.R."

"Thank you," Linda whispered through sobs that for some reason struck me as sounding a little manufactured.

"I just don't know *how* I'm gonna go on without him. Who on earth would *do* such a terrible thing? Everyone *loved* J.R." Linda dragged out her words and sobbed dramatically.

"I'm sure the truth will come out, Linda. We just have to have faith." I assured her, but in my mind the wheels were turning. I don't know who would want J.R. out of the way, but I was about to do my best to find out.

CHAPTER 2

*J*ake and several uniformed officers arrived, followed by the ambulance. Not that there was a big rush. It would be a quiet ride back to the coroner's office. When the coroner finished his assessment of the body, Jake pulled him over to the side and I inched my way as close as I could, straining to overhear the conversation.

"So, when do you estimate the time of death?" Jake asked.

"Recent. No more than an hour, I would say. Weapon looks like it would have been something long, sharp like a knife. Smooth, edge, not serrated. About six inches long, maybe?"

"Like this?" Jake asked, pulling an evidence bag out of his pocket containing my letter opener.

"Exactly like that."

It was at that moment Jake looked up and noticed me conveniently loitering nearby.

"Glory, can I talk to you a minute? I need to get a statement about how you found the body."

"Sure, Jake." I nodded, recounting every detail I could remember about the last hour. "Momma and I were out back at the picnic tables helping Martha Jean put out food and I decided I would go to the car and lock our Bibles and purses away for safekeeping. It was parked on the far side of the graveyard because we were running a little late this morning and there was nowhere else to park. You know how Sunday mornings are. You think you're doing good on time and then all *"you know what"* breaks loose and . . ."

"Ahem . . ." Jake cleared his throat. "Go on," Jake urged with a slight grin because he knew how I could chase a rabbit or two.

"Anyway, I was admiring all the flowers as I walked around the graves when I saw a shoe sticking out from behind the tree." I shivered as I remembered. "I thought it was some kids playing hide and seek or Ghost in the Graveyard. I called out and told them that playing out there was off limits, but the shoe didn't move." I swallowed and continued. "That's when I rounded the tree and saw J.R. just sitting there. I knew right away that he was dead."

"Did you touch anything?"

I shook my head. "No, I know better than that. I watch a lot of detective shows. I just started screaming for Joe and Momma to call you."

"Did you see this on the ground next to him?" Jake asked as he showed me the letter opener.

"Yes. Do you think it's the murder weapon?"

"We won't know for sure, but the coroner said it's possible. I'll have it checked for prints."

"You need to know something," I admitted.

"What's that?" he cocked one eyebrow.

"It's mine." I answered calmly. "My prints will be all over it. I keep it on my desk."

"In the church office?" Jake exclaimed as the fact of that statement registered with him. "Then that means there's a chance he wasn't killed here. We need to get that office secured." He motioned for another officer to cordon off the office area.

"I've already instructed Joe to make sure no one went near it." I proudly announced.

"You did?" Jake eyed me suspiciously. "And just how did you know to do that?"

"Well, I saw the letter opener on the ground and recognized it. I knew it had to come from my office which meant the killer had to have been there at some point. He must have swiped it off my desk and killed J.R. there or followed him out and killed him out here. Either way, it's a secondary crime scene. The back entrance to the church building is actually the front entrance to the church office. It would have been a quick exit to displace the body and buy himself some time to get away."

"What would J.R. have been doing in the church office during the service?"

"Last time I saw him, he was passing the offering plate with the other ushers. I'm sure he was taking the offering to the safe drawer. Oh no!! The offering!" I exclaimed.

"Keep your voice down, Glory. We don't need all these onlookers worrying about that just yet."

"Has anyone checked the safe yet? J.R. would have been headed there to drop the offering in the safe until we can get it deposited tomorrow. There was also a large donation."

Jake jerked his head around. "What kind of donation?"

"Friday morning, Joe Nabors came by the church to drop off a donation. It was $10,000 cash in bank stacks with those paper strips around them. His father passed away recently and left him quite a bit of money. He wanted Pastor Dan to use it where it was needed most. I asked him to watch me place it in the safe before he left."

Jake blew out a low whistle. "That is quite a chunk of money, plus what was probably a pretty big offering total today, with the big crowd and all."

Jake motioned for one of the uniformed officers to come over and I listened while he instructed him to find Pastor Dan to open the safe and see if the money had indeed been dropped by J.R. before the incident and to make sure that the large amount of cash was still there. The officer left in the direction of the church office as Jake turned back to me.

"Glory, I know how much you love your mysteries, but promise me you are not going to try out your mystery-solving skills and stick your nose in this investigation," he warned. "This isn't one of your mystery books. This is the real thing and it could be dangerous."

"You sound just like Momma." I said. "I have no intention of messing up your investigation. But, if I happened to stumble across some tidbit of information that might you help you out, how could that cause any harm?"

Jake cut me a warning look.

I looked him in the eye, "As Granny used to say, 'I'm just here to be a blessing!'"

* * *

Needless to say, dinner on the ground was a bust this year. Once the officers had taken statements they needed, most everyone took their dishes home, still covered in the foil they brought them in. Martha Jean was distraught that no one got to taste her banana pudding cake. Carl got a group of deacons to help tear down all the tables and chairs that had been set up under the trees. All in all, it was a sad ending to what should have been a nice celebration.

Momma, feeling exhausted and distraught from the events of the day, elected to go home to lie down while Macy and I grabbed a very late lunch at Loco Pollo, the little Mexican restaurant that had recently opened out on the highway. It was surprisingly busy for this late in the day, but evidently all the folks who were planning to eat lunch at church had to find somewhere else to go.

The menu was what I liked to call Southern Mexican. These little places are all over the south and all menus read the same. Every place has a list of specials by number and everyone orders a P10, like it's a generic name for a big plate of rice with grilled chicken and white cheese sauce. Like calling all soft drinks, Cokes and all tissues, Kleenex. They call it authentic, but after living in Texas, I realized it's just not the same as the real thing. Nevertheless, it was still yummy and who can pass up chips and salsa? Not this girl.

On the way home, we dropped off the container of French macarons, that were to be Macy's contribution to the potluck, at the police station. Jake could share them with everyone since we knew they'd be working some long hours over the next few days.

Finally pulling into the driveway, I asked Macy, "Are you sure you're alright after all that's happened today? I'm so sorry you had to see all that."

"I'm fine, Mom. Really, I am. What about you? Are you okay?"

"It was definitely a shock seeing a real dead body. I mean, I've watched so many crime shows, I thought I would be immune to it if I ever saw one, but when it's a real person, especially one that you know, it was just terrible."

"Why don't we go in and let's just relax and try to get our mind off of it for awhile."

I reached my arm around Macy's shoulders and hugged her to my side as we walked up the front porch steps. Macy had recently moved in with me temporarily after she finished her master's degree. She had decided to move here instead of accepting a job offer back in Texas with a well-known bakery in the town where she grew up. No matter how temporary, I was happy to have her here with me. Her dream had always been to open her own bakery and with the money she had put away while she was working a part-time job during school plus some of the money from Dave's insurance policy, we were going to make that happen.

We both sat down on the sofa, legs tucked up under us, and started flipping through the channels on TV until we landed on a remodeling show that looked interesting. After a few minutes of watching the stars pull down paneling, I asked Macy, "What kind of things do you have in mind for the interior of the bakery?"

"I've been thinking about that." She shifted on the sofa and sat up straighter. "I'm envisioning that the bakery counter and barista area should be to the left as you enter with several sets of tables and chairs to the right of the staircase. What do you think?"

Closing my eyes, I tried to picture the beautiful area that had once been a furniture store in its heyday. There was the most gorgeous grand staircase in the center of the room. It flared out wider at the bottom and narrowed as it rose to a second-floor loft that ran the entire way around the room overlooking the whole downstairs. There was paneling, circa 1960's on almost every wall but I was sure there was beautiful brick behind it just waiting to be exposed. The ceilings were those beautiful old pressed tin tiles. Some were missing or stained, but that could be remedied. The old scuffed, hardwood floors needed some love and refinishing.

"I think that sounds like a great floorplan. You will get the best flow in and out the front doors and customers who want to sit and visit won't feel like they are in the way of those who are in a hurry to grab and go."

"It is a beautiful building, isn't it Mom?" Macy said, hugging a pillow to chest tightly.

"Yes, it's perfect. It's been several businesses over the years. I'm not sure when the furniture store closed, but I remember it mostly as a fine jewelry store while I was growing up. That must have gone out of business while I was off at college and it seems I remember a craft shop there at one time, but it's been sitting empty for several years now."

"Do you remember when it was filled with furniture?"

"I remember going there when I was a little girl with Granny and Momma to buy some things. I think Granny bought an old wringer type washing machine there and a few other pieces over the years. You know the big four-poster bedroom set that Momma still has in her back bedroom? Granny and Grandaddy actually won that at the grand opening of the store in 1948."

"You're kidding me! I love that bed! This is all so cool."

I could see the excitement bubbling up in Macy's sparkling hazel eyes. The wheels were turning.

"Mom, it has the potential to be a dream bakery and coffee shop. I could even expand to sell kitchen items upstairs like cookbooks and other gifts."

"We have quite a bit of work ahead of us, but it's going to be exactly what you've dreamed of."

Macy smiled as she closed her eyes and leaned her head back on the sofa pillow.

"I think I'm going to turn in. The excitement of the day has finally hit rock bottom and I'm about to crash. I'll see you in the morning, darling."

"Good night, Mom."

CHAPTER 3

Monday morning came way too soon and in my regular routine, I scooted Izzy out of the way, threw off the covers and dragged myself out of the bed. Sliding my feet into my favorite fuzzy, pink flamingo slippers, I wiggled my toes and padded into the kitchen to start the coffee. I could have slept in since Pastor Dan had called late Sunday night to let me know that the church office would be closed for a few days. The investigators were still there and were combing through the office and church property for clues to who could have killed poor J.R. But there's no way I could sleep. Tossing and turning in the bed, I tried to fall asleep, but all I could think about was J.R., Linda, and their sweet baby boy. How hard it must be on her right now and how she was going to have to face the future as a single parent. Macy was practically a grown woman when Dave died, so I can't imagine what a challenge it will be for Linda. I wondered if he had insurance. Was he a good provider?

Would she lose her house? Did she have any family close enough to help her out?

The sight of J.R.'s body leaning against that tree kept playing over and over in my mind. I knew I just had to do whatever I could to help Jake get this solved. I didn't know J.R. well, but surely he didn't deserve this.

With the scent of dark roast beginning to waft through the house, I let Izzy out the back door into the fenced back yard. "Go do your stuff, Izzy, and I'll get your food ready." Izzy snorted and sniffed, did her business and came right back in, wiggling her little nub of a tail for breakfast. I reached into the cabinet and took out my favorite mug and set it on the counter. I breathed in a big whiff of the scent. I'd always loved the smell of coffee, but until about a year ago, I'd never really been much of a coffee drinker. I was always more of a Diet Coke girl, but caffeine is caffeine, anyway you can get it. Macy told me that a person's taste buds change every seven years, so periodically, I would try coffee again. Each time I would just shiver and spit it right back in the mug. Then, one day, like magic, I thought, "this isn't half bad", and I'd been addicted ever since. I poured myself a mug full, added my favorite sugar-free creamer, and sat down at the kitchen table with my Bible for my morning devotion.

"The steadfast love of the Lord never ceases; His mercies never come to an end; they are new every morning; great is Your faithfulness. 'The Lord is my portion', says my soul, 'therefore I will hope in Him.'" Lamentations 3:22-24

A lot had changed in my life in the last year. One split

second in time had changed my life forever and I would never be the same again. Losing the love of my life had left a huge hole in my heart, but couple that with the inconceivable shock of discovering that for the last ten years of our thirty year marriage, my husband, Dave, had been living a double life as a covert agent for the government was almost more than I could handle. I had known Dave since ninth grade, but had I ever really known him at all? I still wrestled with feeling anger toward him for lying to me all those years and then the next minute feeling pride that he worked trying to right wrongs and put criminals behind bars. It left me in a mess of conflicted emotions many days. He was a certified public accountant for Pete's sake. How could that have been dangerous? It was something that had taken me months to process. Truth be known, I was still in that process, but after months of trying to convince the police to keep investigating, I knew all the demanding and nagging in the world was never going to change their minds. Not without new evidence and no one seemed to be interested in looking for that. I finally had to come to the realization that the best thing for me to do was to try to move forward. I knew without a doubt that Dave would not have wanted me to stop living my life. I had to be there for Macy and to keep our family intact. Had I done the right thing? It was hard. Harder than I ever thought possible. Moving from Texas, where we had lived for thirty years, back home to Sweetwater Springs six months ago was a big step in the right direction. I knew that it was time for a change and a fresh start, getting back to my roots and to a place and people I loved, and I knew loved me. Izzy nudged my leg and I blinked back the tears welling up in my eyes. Shaking my head, I straightened up and took a deep breath. "Glory Harper, you know God's got this. This is a new day and His mercies are new! Let's get moving, Izzy."

I was lost in my thoughts when I heard the sound of a door close and for a split second, my heart jumped in my chest. I was still getting used to the sounds of someone else in the house. It took me months to get used to the deathly quiet of being alone after Dave was killed. But the sound of the shower running in the hall bath was a comforting sound. At first, I felt guilty when Macy told me that she wanted to move home to Sweetwater Springs after she finished her master's degree. I was convinced that she was putting her own life on hold and only moving back for my sake. But after much discussion, she convinced me that it wasn't a compromise. It was her dream, too. With her culinary degree and a masters in restaurant management, her dream had always been to own her own bakery and we knew we had found the perfect location. It was prime storefront property on Main Street, and we got it for a steal. Sure, there was a lot of work to be done before it would open, but for the first time in a long time, I was excited for the future.

I was doing my best to give Macy her own space and not to hover. She had been on her own for a few years now and I didn't want it to be awkward while she's back in the house.

My cell phone buzzed with an incoming call. I saw Jake's name and answered.

"Good morning, Jake."

"Good morning, Sis. How are you this morning? Did you get any sleep last night?"

"Not much. Every time I closed my eyes, I saw J.R. sitting there. Jake, you just have to find out who did this to him. Do you have any suspects yet?"

"Actually, that's why I'm calling. I'm gonna need you to come down to the station this morning, give us your fingerprints and answer a few more questions."

"Jake, surely I'm not a suspect! You know I could never hurt someone like that!"

"I'm just doing my job, Sis. Please don't take it personally. I need your fingerprints on file to compare to the ones that will be on the letter opener."

"Don't take it personally?" My voice raised at least two octaves. "How else am I supposed to take my brother practically accusing me of murder?"

"Don't be so dramatic. You know I have to rule you out as a suspect. Even though you had opportunity and your prints are on the murder weapon, I don't think you had a motive, did you?"

"What do you mean I had opportunity? I was in the service up until Momma and I went out to help Martha Jean."

"The coroner's report just came back and he puts time of death between 11:45 and noon. You said that you and Mom slipped out of the service during the offertory. I checked with Pastor Dan and he had been watching the clock on the pulpit closely during the service to make sure he kept on schedule and that the offertory began precisely at 11:40. I talked to Martha Jean and she said that Mom came out first, but you came out several minutes later. Where did you go when you left the service?"

"Oh, shoot! I went by the ladies' room. I had forgotten about that. It couldn't have taken me more than a few minutes."

"Is there anything else you might have forgotten to mention? I know you were probably in shock yesterday. Maybe you've remembered other details that would help me?"

"I don't think there's anything else, but I'll think about it and let you know when I come by the station. I'm sorry I snapped at you, Jake. This whole thing just really has me on edge. Since the office is closed and I can't go into work, I thought I'd head over to Momma's to see what she's doing today."

Jake knew that Momma and I together with a whole day off could mean trouble and mischief. Last time we spent the whole day together, my hair was bobbed off and Momma's toenails were painted hot pink. "Well, just keep your nose out of things that don't concern you," he warned, "and I'll see you down here in about a half an hour."

"Yes, sir." I agreed and smiled to myself, knowing that anything that happened in my office definitely concerned me, so I wasn't really telling a fib.

I didn't know J.R. and Linda all that well. They were much younger than me and I'd lost track of a lot of people while I was living in Texas. They were members of the church and Linda seemed like such a sweet thing. I knew I really wanted to help. Not to mention that the killer used my letter opener to do the unspeakable. I had to make sure that my name was marked off that suspect list as soon as possible and if that meant doing a little snooping to help Jake out, then so be it. No one should get away with such a terrible thing.

J.R. was the head usher and in charge of what was probably a larger than usual offering that morning. Was that the motive? Was it a drifter looking for quick cash? Joe Nabors' large donation was also in the safe. Had someone somehow gotten wind of that? I had forgotten to ask Jake if the offering was still in the safe drawer. I would ask him when I got to the station.

After a quick shower, I blew my shoulder-length brown hair dry and tried to give it enough lift with hairspray to keep it out of my eyes for the day. I envied Macy who had inherited her daddy's curls. My hair was straight as a fireplace poker just like Momma's. I was also noticing a few straggler gray hairs here and there. Another thing I knew I'd inherited from Momma. I tapped on the hall bathroom door and Macy emerged with a towel around her head and a smile that warmed my heart from the inside out.

"Mornin' Mom!", Macy chirped as she tightened the bathrobe around her waist.

I hugged her goodbye with a promise to check in with her later in the morning.

CHAPTER 4

The police station, located in an old brick building, was in the center of town at the intersection of Main Street and Sheffield. It was built in the sixties and still had that mid-century vibe I usually loved in old buildings. I walked through the double glass doors and was immediately met by the scent of burnt coffee and musty old files. The lady behind the desk looked up from her computer monitor. "Can I help you?"

"Yes, I'm here to see Jake Miller." I beamed my most innocent smile.

"He's not here. Are you his sister?" She responded grumpily, eyeing me over the top of her cat eye reading glasses.

"Yes, Glory Harper."

"He had to run an errand and said for you to speak with Chief Detective Walker. His office is straight back, first door on the left." She said, jabbing the pen she was holding in the air in the direction of a long, wood-paneled hall.

I was absolutely frustrated with Jake for not being here after he told me to come down, and now he makes me talk with some stodgy old guy who probably hasn't seen the outside of his office in years. I stalked down the dimly lit hall and tapped on the door frame of an open doorway. "Chief Detective Walker? I'm Glory Harper. Jake . . . I mean Detective Miller, asked me to speak with you."

"Mrs. Harper, Hunt Walker. Please, sit down." The man who stood to greet me was not what I expected. His demeanor was all business, but not curt. He was middle aged, fit and actually *quite* handsome.

He directed me to the only other chair in the small office and he took a seat behind a cluttered desk and started shuffling through a collection of file folders.

"I know you have already given your statement to the officers, but could you recount your actions of yesterday morning for me, just for my benefit?" He said without even looking up from his file.

For the umpteenth time, I told what I could remember about Sunday's events. This time, I did remember to include the fact that I stopped by the ladies' room on the way out to the lunch tables.

"Which restroom did you use?"

"I went into the one just outside the door to the sanctuary."

"Are there other restrooms in the building?"

"Yes, there's one down the back hall near the church office and then one over in the preschool area."

"Did you see anyone else in the restroom while you were in there?"

"No. As far as I remember, there was no one else. In

fact, I remember specifically checking the stalls, because several were out of toilet paper." I'm not sure why I cared, but I felt my cheeks blush at the subject of our discussion.

"I see." I saw his square jaw twitch like he was trying to hold back a grin. "I think that will be all for now. I need you to stop by the processing desk to leave your fingerprints so that we can rule you out as a suspect. Jake assures me that you barely knew the victim and, to his knowledge, had no motive. We will leave it at that unless evidence presents a need to take a closer look at you. Thank you again for your time." He said as he stood and looked at me with gray blue eyes that looked like they could see right through me. Obviously, it was time for me to leave and I was never so glad to get out of a room in my life.

I stopped short of the door and turned back to the desk. "Can you tell me if the church safe was checked and if the money from the offering as well as the large amount of cash was still in it?"

He looked up at me with a look of a surprise. "I'm sorry, I'm not at liberty to discuss an ongoing investigation."

"You see," I ignored his statement and continued, "I'm the one who placed the donation in the safe and I can't help but feel responsible for its safety."

He nodded as if to understand my reasoning. "I understand. Unfortunately, the offering hasn't been located, but the cash donation was still inside the safe."

"Oh, so I guess that means that the killer must have been waiting on J.R. and got to him before he could reach the safe room in the back of the office. I hope we can recover the offering intact, because that will be an accounting nightmare trying to notify those who put money in the plate. But I am thankful that the larger donation was still there."

"Yes, *we* will do our best to recover anything in that bank bag." I thought I saw the corners of his mouth turn up the least little bit. Maybe he didn't think I was a murderer, after all.

"Thank you." I walked out the door and let out the breath I didn't realize I'd been holding. I couldn't decide if I liked that guy or not, but hopefully, that would be my last encounter with him anyway.

After stopping by the police station, I went straight to Momma's. I knocked on the back door and Momma waved me on in. The smell of bacon and eggs made my stomach rumble. I loved my momma's kitchen. It was always so cozy and homey. She lived in the family home that had belonged to my grandparents. The walls were lined with vintage enameled metal cabinets and pine paneling. The ceiling was covered in exposed, painted shiplap. Very retro and very desirable these days. HGTV and Pinterest had taught everyone how to give old things new life. Not that Momma cared about being "in style", she just loved her home the way it was.

"Good morning, Momma!" I said as I grabbed a pitcher of sweet tea out of the fridge, poured myself a glass and sat down at the table.

"Mornin', Glory!"

Everyone got such a kick out of greeting me that way, Momma included. She was standing over a skillet full of bacon, a hot pink apron tied around her waist. Momma's blue eyes stood out against her salt and pepper gray hair. I had always thought Momma was beautiful. Even if she did wear eyeglasses that were ten years out of style and held together at the nosepiece by duct tape. I laughed at the sight of them. "Momma, when are you going to get some new glasses? I don't know how you see out of those old things!"

"I can see better out of these than my new ones. I'm never going back to that eye doctor again," she stated definitively.

"How are you doing after all the craziness at the church yesterday?" I took a long drink of my tea and sighed.

"I'm still a little shook up," Momma admitted. "In fact, I'm more than a little mad that something like that can happen right under our noses, in our town and in God's house!" She poured herself a big mug of coffee, added a shot of creamer and sat down at the table across from me.

"I know, I feel the same way. That's why I came over. I just wanted to talk through some things with you." I said as I reached into my purse and pulled out my notepad and pencil.

"What do you have there?" Momma's eyes got wide. "Gloria Lynn Miller! What do you think you're doing with that list?"

Uh oh. I knew when I heard my full name, Momma was serious, so I braced myself for what was about to come.

Momma cocked her eyebrow and breathed out a long, consigned sigh, "I'm in. How can I help?"

I didn't see that coming, but I jumped at the chance to get Momma's input.

"Well, for starters, I didn't really know J.R. that well, so tell me anything you can about him. Who did he spend time with? Where did he hang out? Anything you know about his relationships. That kind of thing. The bakery was listed By Owner when Macy bought it, so we didn't really have a need for a real estate agent."

"I don't know a lot about his private life, but I did hear something interesting this week from Bonnie down at the beauty shop."

Bonnie June Dixon owned Bonnie's Cut and Curl right next door to Sweetwater Springs Realty on Main Street. The salon was a hotbed of gossip and interesting conversations.

"Bonnie said that J.R. and his business partner, Terrance Wolfe, had a knockdown, drag out fight in front of the real estate office Saturday morning. The door to Bonnie's salon was propped open and she heard every word. She heard Terrance saying something about wanting to move to a bigger office and expand the business and how J.R. was a small-timer with no vision. J.R. accused him of trying to take over the business. She said it almost came to blows!"

"Yikes! That sounds pretty serious." I said. "I heard that Terrance just bought a nice house on the lake, so the business must be doing well. I guess he's wanting it to turn into more and it sounds like J.R. is happy with the way things are. You know, some people can be satisfied with a lot less and some people just always gotta have more."

"You're right. The Bible says, '...*the love of money is the*

root of all evil.'" Momma quoted. "I just hope those roots
stay out of our town."

"I think the best place for us to start is with Linda." I
said, still formulating a plan in my head. "Do you think
she'll talk to us?"

Momma's eyes lit up. "I've got an idea. I have everything I need in the pantry to make a dish of funeral potatoes. Why don't we throw those together and take them
by her house?"

"Perfect! Food will get you in the door every time."

Funeral potatoes is a dish that will make you slap your
grandma. Hashbrown potatoes mixed with all kinds of
cheese made for a delicious dish. It was a well-known fact
that Momma was one of the best cooks in town. Since she
never got remarried after Daddy died, she lived alone, but
she was always looking for any reason to cook something
for somebody. I guess the cooking gene skipped a generation, because I surely didn't get it. I was just thankful that
Macy did.

I helped Momma collect all the ingredients for the
casserole out of the pantry and we made quick work of
the yummy dish. As the oven dinged, Momma took it out
and placed it in a hot dish carrier. It filled the house with
the smell of cheesy potato goodness. I took in a deep
breath, "This will definitely get us in the door."

* * *

Sweetwater Springs wasn't a booming Alabama
metropolis, so there weren't a lot of people busting down
the doors to move here. In fact, there wasn't even a full-

blown traffic light. Just a flashing red light out on the highway in front of the Piggly Wiggly. After the trailer plants shut down, the economy went with them, but the beauty of the area and the people made it worth staying. The trailer plants, or the mobile and modular home industry as they preferred to be known, had been a big chunk of the economy around the county for as long as I could remember. A few years back, they started moving their factories to other towns, one by one, and pretty soon Sweetwater Springs was in dire straits.

But, despite its economic lull, it was a beautiful little town steeped in a proud history. During the days leading up to the Civil War, the county seceded from the state of Alabama in an effort to remain neutral in the conflict. There was even a statue erected in the town square of a soldier that is half Union and half Confederate to commemorate the divided loyalties during the war.

The biggest draw, though, was Smith Lake. It was a huge, beautiful lake stretching into three counties. Sitting right in the middle of the beautiful Bankhead National Forest, it really did have so much to offer. When you grow up in a town, sometimes you take for granted all the things at your fingertips. Things you saw as a way of life, others would actually pay good money to enjoy. Smith Lake was one of those things. It had something for everyone with loads of water sports and a great little restaurant and family-owned motel. The shoreline was lined with everything from travel campers to gated mansions. It seemed to me that J.R. and Terrance had built Sweetwater Springs Realty into a nice little business. Lakefront property was at a premium and there were people who lived elsewhere that owned a place on the lake and just spent the summer here. I had spent countless high school days with friends laying out on the dock at the marina or out on Kelly's family's ski boat. Yes, Sweet-water Springs has always been a nice, safe town. I was afraid that was beginning to change.

CHAPTER 5

J.R. and Linda lived just out of town, about five miles down the highway towards the lake. The modest, ranch style home was neatly kept with a small front yard. Flower beds flanked each side of the steps leading up to the front door. They were filled with petunias, lantana and daylilies.

Momma knocked on the door as I stood by holding the still warm invitation to snoop.

Linda answered the door, her eyes red-rimmed and her hair pulled back in a clip. She smiled, "Come in, ladies. How thoughtful of you both to come by. That smells delicious."

"Should I take this on to the kitchen?" I asked, glancing through the living area to what looked like the kitchen.

"Yes, please do. Thank you. Annie, won't you have a seat." I heard her say to Momma as I continued on to the kitchen.

Walking through, I took the opportunity to look around the living and dining rooms. Admiring several pictures in frames on the mantel, on the old upright piano and on the walls, something odd occurred to me. None of them --- not one of them --- had J.R in it. They were all of Linda, their little boy or extended family members and friends. Maybe he just didn't like posing for pictures or maybe he was the photographer in the family.

I walked on into the kitchen and seeing a trivet on the countertop, I removed the dish from the carrier and placed it on there. I could see from the kitchen window a pretty little backyard with a playset. Glancing around the kitchen for anything that might be a clue, I opened drawer after drawer. Spices. Dish towels. Junk drawer. Everybody has one. Nothing out of the ordinary in there.

"Can I help you find something?" a voice came from behind me and I jumped.

"Oh! Yes, ma'am. I was looking for a serving spoon for these potatoes," I said as my heart skipped a beat.

"Here's one," she said opening a different drawer. "I'm Linda's mom, Connie. Thank you for the food and for your thoughtfulness."

"You're more than welcome. This is all so sad. J.R. seemed like such a nice man."

Connie looked at me. "Looks can be deceiving." She turned on her heel and walked out. Taken aback by such a blunt comment, I followed her. As I walked past the refrigerator, I saw a piece of paper held up with a magnet on the door. *Sam Baylor 325-9956.* Probably nothing, but I snapped a quick picture with my phone and rejoined the others in the other room.

"Mom, this is Annie Miller and her daughter, Glory Harper. We all go to church together and Glory is the church secretary." Linda introduced and Connie nodded a solemn greeting.

"Linda, this is all such a shock. We are just so sorry. I'm so glad you have your Mom here with you and your son at a time like this. Families are such a blessing."

Linda nodded. "Matthew doesn't understand any of this. He's so young. That will be his saving grace, I think. That while he may have some vague memories of J.R. lingering, he will be able to handle it pretty well. Kids are resilient."

"I'm sure it will take awhile, but he will be fine with you and your mom here. Do you have any idea who might have done this? Did J.R. have any enemies?" Momma asked, patting Linda's hand.

"No one. I know he and Terrance had a disagreement last week, but surely nothing that would lead to this."

"We heard about that. Do you know what it was about?" I asked.

"Terrance has really been pushing J.R. to expand the business into rental properties. He had been on the lookout for prime lakefront property to build some condos for vacation rentals. He said he'd found the perfect deal and was pushing J.R. hard to agree."

"And J.R. wasn't on board with that idea?" I jumped in with another question.

"He felt like it was taking a big financial risk and a lot of debt to take on. We don't have the kind of money that Terrance does. He's single and has no family to support. It's easier for him to take chances with his money."

"I see." I acknowledged, noticing that Connie rolled

her eyes and looked away. *"What was that about?"*, I wondered.

"Are you going to be OK financially after this? I mean. . . did he have insurance? Funeral expenses can be such a financial strain. I know when Glory's father passed away, it took me awhile to replace savings." Momma interjected.

I could see Connie was getting more and more fidgety as she clenched and unclenched her fists. Linda stared blankly at the floor.

Just then, Connie interrupted. "If you must know, he didn't leave her one red cent. He was flat broke. He was a lazy bum who stomped around here like he was Lord of the Manor and slapped his wife around when she didn't answer his beck and call!" Her eyes got wide and her hand flew to her mouth. She got up and ran from the room in tears.

Momma and I looked at Linda, who was still staring at the floor not saying a word. That was definitely our cue to leave.

"Well . . . ummm . . . we need to be going." I said as we stood. "Please call us if you need anything at all."

Linda nodded and we let ourselves out.

Momma got into the car and buckled her seatbelt. "Well that was more than a little awkward."

"Yes, it was," I said, "but I think we got some useful information and I think we just got the first name to add to our suspect list."

"What's our next move?" Momma's eyes were brimming with excitement.

"Momma, you are enjoying this way too much." I said.

"Oh please, don't think I'm heartless. I really do feel

terrible for poor Linda and Matthew, but I have to admit this is the biggest adventure I've had in years!"

"Let's head back into town. I'll call Kelly and see if she can come meet us for a quick lunch at Moody's."

Kelly was the director of our local library and she seemed to love it. She always had her nose in a book when we were kids. She was the one that got me hooked on reading murder mysteries. She had always been inquisitive and loved a good puzzle. One of our favorite things to do growing up was to read the same mystery book and have a contest to see who could solve the crime the fastest. We called it the Crime Club. Even now, we still continued the Crime Club tradition when new releases from our favorite authors came out.

At first, Kelly thought her degree in Computer Science would be wasted working in a library, but I quickly reassured her that so much online research is done there and she is the perfect one to help the novice when they are at their wit's end. She really was a wiz on the computer. She could find any information you need in no time flat.

I also texted Macy to see if she wanted to meet us, but she was still pulling paneling off the walls at the bakery and was waiting on a flooring guy to come by for a quote.

After ordering a couple of burger combos, Momma and I sat down to wait on our food. Kelly breezed in and pulled up a chair to the table.

"Aren't you going to eat?" I asked, taking a sip of my drink.

"No, I'm just grabbing a sweet tea. I have a big group of children coming to the library this afternoon for story time and I need to get back."

"How's your new assistant working out?"

"She has been heaven sent! With her help, we've been able to work through those stacks of books that were donated last month. She's already got them labeled and shelved."

We all settled into our seats and I pulled out my phone and scrolled through the pictures.

"While I was in Linda's kitchen, I found this phone number stuck to her refrigerator door. It could be nothing, but for some reason, that name sounds so familiar to me. Do either of you recognize it?" I passed the phone to both of them. Both ladies thought for just a minute and agreed that it didn't ring a bell with either of them.

"Sam Baylor, Sam Baylor . . . why does that name sound so familiar?" I was straining my brain trying to recall where I had heard it. "I remember! That's the name of the young man who called the church last week looking for J.R. and Linda. I guess he found them." I exclaimed. "With all that's happened, I had totally forgotten about taking that call. He said he was an old college friend and asked if I knew them. I guess he was able to reconnect with them after all."

"Glory, you didn't give out a member's private information did you?" Momma gasped.

"I didn't give him a phone number or home address. I did tell him where J.R.'s office was." I froze. "Oh no! What if he's the killer! What have I done? This may all be my fault!"

"Now honey, don't you think that." Kelly patted the back of my hand as I was beginning to panic.

"You didn't do anything wrong. You didn't give him

any information he wouldn't have gotten from Joe Blow on the street if he had asked. Everyone knows where the realty office is." Momma consoled and I began to breathe a little easier.

"Now that I think about it, that must have been him sitting with J.R. Sunday morning for a short time. I remember he got up and slipped out just before J.R. got up to help with the offering."

The waitress, dressed in khakis and a putrid yellow polo shirt with a red arched M on the left front, placed our baskets of burgers and fries down in front of us. I felt bad for the employees having to wear those shirts. That color doesn't look good on anybody. It made them all look like they should be treated for jaundice. Kelly eyed our burger baskets enviously. She had never had to worry about putting on an ounce of weight while I, on the other hand, could smell food and gain ten pounds.

We said the blessing over our food and I could tell Kelly was about to burst to tell us something. I practically saw the light bulb go on over her head.

"Wait a minute! It just came to me. I do recognize that name! He came into the library last Friday researching some local land ownership. I helped him pull up public records."

"Whose records was he looking for?"

"Let me think," Kelly tapped her fingers on the table. "Charles Lindsey and Judith Lindsey, I believe. Yes, I think they were father and daughter. He said they had owned land here at one time and wanted to find out if it was still in their name or if they had sold it. Said he might be inheriting it soon."

"So maybe his real reason for visiting Sweetwater Springs was to find the land and the visit to the Jenkins was just that . . . a short little visit to say hello."

Kelly glanced down at her watch. "I'm sorry to drink and run, but I really need to get back to work," she scooted her chair away from the table. "After the children's story time this afternoon, maybe I'll have time to get online and dig a little into the Lindsey family and Sam Baylor."

"That's a great idea!" I agreed. "Why don't you come over tonight and you can fill me in on what you find and we'll order some pizza."

"That sounds perfect!"

Since I'd moved back from Texas, Kelly and I had made it a point to schedule a supper date once a week. We usually alternated houses and this would have been Kelly and Jake's week, but with the murder investigation, I knew that she and Jake wouldn't need the extra stress, so I figured I would offer to host. After all this is over and done, Kelly could do two weeks in a row. Truth be told, I loved entertaining. Now that Macy was here, maybe she could give me some cooking lessons and I could do a little more of it.

"While I'm thinking about it, how about supper at our house tomorrow night? I know it's technically your week to host, but since Jake is so tied up with the investigation, let's do it at our house."

"Oh, that actually works out better," Kelly agreed. "With the murder, Jake is really swamped.

"I'll see you this afternoon around 5:30," she said gathering her things and waved as she walked out.

CHAPTER 6

I turned to Momma, "Are you in a huge rush to get home?"

"No plans. What do you have in mind?"

"Do you mind if we run by Busy Bee? I need to place an order for the altar flowers for next Sunday. Since I didn't work today, I totally forgot that was on my Monday to-do list. I don't have my reminders in front of me and I just don't want to forget something important."

It was a glorious day, so we decided to walk down to the other end of Main Street, browsing in the shop windows that dotted both sides of the street. Even with all the revitalization, there were still a few that sat empty. Busy Bee Flowers was a cute little shop two doors down from the old furniture store. It was one of the first shops to move in and had been an inspiration for several others to help revitalize the downtown area. It had a black and white striped awning across the front. The big window had the logo with a cute bee buzzing around a big yellow and white daisy. The inside was just as cute. The concrete floors had been stripped, stained and polished with a glossy coat. The walls were all shiplap and painted a clean, farmhouse white. Wreaths and arrangements hung on every wall with shelves all spaced throughout the store with gifts of all kinds. Scented candles added to the wonderful floral smells. There were wooden signs and other home accents. There was even a baby gift section toward the back with loads of cute baby gifts. My favorite area was the kitchen section with a selection of mixes for yummy dips and cheese balls. I loved to keep those on hand for tailgating during football season.

"I think I'll pick up this mix for Blueberry Cream Cheese Dip for Rummy Club tomorrow night. It'll be quick and easy." Momma picked up a couple of the packets and kept shopping.

While she browsed, I placed the order for the church arrangement. Brigette, the owner and the "B" in Busy Bee, greeted me. "Hi, Glory! How have you been doing? I'll bet it's been crazy at your office after what happened to J.R. Jenkins."

"That's why I stopped by. The office is closed today and tomorrow because of the investigation and I almost forgot to order the altar flowers for Sunday. Can you deliver a large arrangement early Sunday morning? Just make it nice and "springy". I know it will be beautiful."

"Absolutely! And I'll put it on the church account." She jotted down the information for the order as she continued. "Speaking of J.R., have you talked to Linda? How is she doing? I heard her ex is in town."

"Her ex?" I know I looked confused.

"Yeah, Sam Baylor. I guess I shouldn't call him an ex. I

don't think they ever officially dated, but he sure had a thing for her before she married J.R."

I moved in closer so any other customers wouldn't overhear our conversation. "Are you good friends with Linda?"

"Yes, we graduated together. She's such a sweet person. We have become pretty close over the last year. I always hated that she married J.R. He treated her badly in high school and from what I hear, it hasn't gotten any better. She mentioned that he has even hit her and little Matthew a few times."

"So sad," I said, shaking my head. "Is there anything else that you can tell me that might help point the police in the right direction? Anything at all?" I asked looking around to make sure no one else could hear.

"Are you helping Jake with the investigation?" Brigette looked confused.

"Let's just say that I am collecting any bits of information I might come across that might help him solve the murder." I conveniently left out the part about Jake telling me to stay out of it.

Brigette looked as if she was trying to decide if she should share information. "Can we step into the back room for a minute?"

I looked over at Momma and put up a single finger to let her know I'd be right back.

"I would normally never share information given to me in confidence, but I think Jake should know. Linda told me that Sam showed up last week at the realty office out of the blue. He was in town to check out some land his family owns. J.R. was out of the office with a client, so he hung around and shot the bull with Terrance and Jeannie until J.R. got back."

"Who is Jeannie?"

"She's the receptionist for the realty office. Anyway, J.R. walked in and they talked for a bit and he invited Sam home for supper. He said Linda was fixing a pot roast and there would be plenty."

"So he went home with J.R. to eat supper and surprised Linda?" I prodded her along.

"Yep, and that's when it started getting good. Linda said she about fainted when she seen him."

"She *saw* him." I corrected. Out came the grammar police. I bit my tongue. While I was living in Texas, people always poked fun at me about my Alabama accent. I didn't realize how much of it I had lost until I moved back home. Texans were southern, but Alabamians were a whole other breed of southern drawl. I loved my Alabama heritage and the slow way we talked and all the southern sayings, but there's a big difference in southern slang and bad grammar. If there's one thing that grated on my nerves, it's people that talk like hicks from the sticks. I tried really hard to rein in the crazy when I heard bad grammar, but sometimes I opened my mouth and my Momma came out.

"That's what I said. She seen him." Brigette continued. "You see, the week before their wedding three years ago, Linda started getting cold feet and Sam had been there for her in the wrong place at the wrong time; or the right place at the right time, if you get what I mean." Brigette cocked her eyebrow and winked. "She had tried to put her feelings for Sam out of her head, but after three years, she said they all came rushing back when he walked through that door."

"You mean . . . they got together before the wedding and . . . oh my!" My hand flew to my mouth.

"That's not all. After our special-called choir practice Friday night, I was the last one in the building, so I was double checking all the doors and turning off lights. I seen Sam and Linda in the parking lot having what looked like a very intimate discussion. He even kissed her."

I bit my tongue again. "This gives Sam a huge motive if I've ever heard one," I said.

I heard the bell on the door jingle and knew Brigette needed to get back up front. We walked from the back to see Linda and her mother walking in.

Momma cleared her throat and placed her items on the counter. "I guess I need to pay for these and we probably need to get going," she glanced at me.

"Hello, Linda. . . Connie. How are you doing?" I greeted her softly, feeling a little awkward after how our last conversation had ended.

"Pretty good, I guess. We just came in to pick out the flowers for J.R.'s casket," she said as tears welled up in her eyes. "I'm sorry, it still just doesn't seem real."

"I completely understand. Please remember that you can call me or Pastor Dan if there's anything that the church can do to help." I said and she nodded.

Brigette rang up Momma's purchase and thanked us and we headed out the door. Since we were only a couple doors down from the bakery, we decided to make a quick stop in to say hello to Macy. She was in the back of the room taking a break at one of the work tables and talking on her phone. She hadn't seen us come in, but I could see her smiling and laughing with whoever was on the other end of the line. She looked up and saw us, waving us on back as she disconnected the call. I fought the urge to ask who she was talking to. *Stop hovering, Glory.*

"Hey, girlie! We were at the flower shop down the street and thought we'd see how it's going. It looks like you have gotten a lot done. Look at all this beautiful brick! And the floors look like they will be in great shape after a good refinishing!"

"I'm pleased with how it's looking so far. I'm just frustrated having to wait around on all these contractor guys. They must live by a different schedule than the rest of us."

"I'm taking Momma home and then I'll see you at the house later."

"Sounds good." Macy said. "I'm about finished pulling down paneling for today so I'll be there as soon as I can get these loose ends tied up."

* * *

Pulling into Momma's driveway, I filled her in on what Brigette had told me. "I guess we know why Sam was so determined to find J.R. and Linda that he would call a random church office to ask for their information. He must still be in love with Linda. This is definitely motive for wanting J.R. out of the way."

"I think maybe tomorrow we should go by Sweetwater Realty and talk to Terrance," Momma said thinking out loud as she got out of the car. "Maybe he can tell us a little more about this land Sam was looking for. You know Sam must have mentioned it to Terrance or J.R. while he was in town since they are realtors."

"I'll see you in the morning and let you know what Kelly finds out online about Sam and the property."

Turning onto our street, I saw that Macy's SUV wasn't in the driveway, so I knew she was still tied up at the bakery. I texted her and told her to join us for pizza as soon as she could get away.

I had been gone since breakfast and I knew Izzy was ready for company. I walked in the front door and was greeted by the sound of tapping little feet bounding down the hall. Izzy jumped up into my arms. "Hello, sweet baby!" I laughed through the onslaught of face licks. "How about we go for a quick walk?" Her wiggling little tail signaled that she was ready to go.

She'd been cooped up in the house all day and needed to stretch her legs and get some fresh air. I clipped the leash to Izzy's collar and headed down the sidewalk. Maybe some fresh air would clear my head, too.

As I walked, taking time to wave at neighbors that were out in their yards or getting their mail, I tried to focus on my suspect list and who else might have had a reason to want J.R. dead.

Izzy and I made the block and, on the way back, I thought about all I had learned today and what Kelly and I might find out tonight. I pulled out my cell phone and selected Buster's Pizza Palace from the speed dial list. I took the mail from the mailbox at the end of the driveway and ordered a large thin crust supreme and an order of cheesy breadsticks as I walked in the front door.

I still needed to talk to Terrance and maybe, Jeannie.

That would be first on the agenda for tomorrow. I would have a full day to investigate, but surely the crime scene would be cleared and the church office would be back open for business as usual on Wednesday. J.R.'s funeral service was scheduled for two o'clock at the church on Wednesday afternoon.

CHAPTER 7

*B*uster's was right on time, just as Kelly was pulling into the driveway. I paid and tipped the delivery guy and set the pizza and cheesy bread on the kitchen counter.

"Ooooh, this smells divine! I'm starving!" Kelly exclaimed. She took a few paper plates and napkins out of the caddy on the kitchen counter as I poured us both a tall glass of sweet tea. Kelly had picked up the cute little caddy as a gift for me while she and Jake were on vacation in the Smoky Mountains a few years ago. It was perfect to hold plates, napkins and plastic utensils. You could even take it outside to the patio for a summertime meal.

Macy walked in and closed her eyes, inhaling the smell of cheese and pepperoni. She quickly washed up and grabbed a plate and a glass of tea to join us.

We took a deep breath and enjoyed really relaxing for the first time since the chaos after church on Sunday. Sitting on the sofa with our feet tucked up under us, I took out my notepad and we talked through the suspect list. Turning to a fresh sheet of paper, I drew out a chart with two columns labeled *motive* and *opportunity*. I listed the suspect names down the left side of the paper.

"Hey, wait a minute! Are you two doing what I think you're doing? Is this a meeting of a real-life version of the Crime Club?" Macy's eyes sparkled with anticipation.

"We just thought we might talk through some possibilities. You know, just to help Jake out." I smiled.

"Can I help too?" Macy asked.

"Of course, you can, but we have to be careful to stay out of Jake's way and not do anything that might mess with his investigation. Got it?"

Macy nodded. "Wait, I think I have a cork board in my room. Would that help us organize everything?"

"That's a great idea. I'll get my pad of sticky notes and some pens."

Macy came back with the board and propped it against the fireplace hearth. I began to write the names of each person connected to the investigation on a sticky note so that we could visualize how they might be connected.

"I think right now, our number one suspect has to be Sam. We saw him slip out of church right before J.R. got up to take the offering, so he had the opportunity and, Lord knows, he has motive." I filled them in on all Brigette had told me this afternoon about Sam and Linda's brief fling and also about our visit with Linda and her mom this morning.

Macy plucked a piece of pepperoni off the pizza slice

and popped it in her mouth. "So according to Brigette, Linda still has feelings for Sam. Do you think he's still in love with her too?"

"I think it's possible. Why else would he go to this much trouble to reconnect with them after three years?"

They both agreed and I put a check mark in both columns next to Sam's name.

"Terrance also has a strong motive, wanting the business to himself, but I'm not sure if he had opportunity."

Motive. Check.

"He's not a regular attender at church, but that doesn't mean he couldn't have slipped in and out without being seen. We had such a large crowd."

I put a question mark in the opportunity column.

"Speaking of the large crowd," Kelly said swallowing a mouth full of cheesy bread, "I just thought about the fact that the offering would have probably been much larger than our normal Sunday offering. Do we know if the money was taken?"

"Detective Walker told me that the bank bag containing the offering, the one J.R. would have been going to drop in the safe, was still missing, but that the cash in the safe was still there."

"Oh no. I really hate that someone took money donated to the church! That's really the lowest of the low." Kelly said thoughtfully. "Well, I guess killing the person you took it from would actually be the lowest, but it's way down there!"

Her reasoning might be a little skewed, but her heart was in the right place.

"There had been a very large donation dropped off at the office on Friday that I locked in the safe. But the killer either wasn't aware of it or they were interrupted before they could get around to taking it. I don't know how anyone could know about it though. I was the only person that even knew it was there, aside from the person who gave it to me. I guess it's possible, though. We can't rule anything out at this point."

"The fact that they took the bank bag from J.R. makes it seem that robbery could have been the reason for the attack, but it's also possible that it was only taken as an afterthought to make it look like a robbery." Macy added.

"I agree. Detective Walker said they were keeping an open mind and investigating all possibilities." I tapped the pencil on my pad and wrote random robber as the suspect and put check marks in both columns and make a sticky note and added it to the board.

"You met Detective Walker?" Kelly's eyes widened. "What did you think of him?"

"Wait! Who is Detective Walker?" Macy shifted on the sofa and looked wide-eyed at me.

"He's Jake's new boss. Jake was out when I went down this morning to leave my fingerprints and so they directed me to him. Actually, I think until I am completely cleared and no longer considered a suspect, Jake will have to take a back seat in this investigation. I guess this new guy is going to head it up. And in answer to your question, Kelly, I thought he was pretty nice and all business."

"No, Glory. I mean what did you *think* of him?" she said with a waggle of her eyebrows. "He's kind of a stud, don't you think?"

I felt my cheeks flush. "I guess he is kind of nice look-ing. If you go for that fit, salt and pepper kind of look."

"Mom! You're blushing! You think he's hot, don't you?" Macy fell over on the sofa laughing.

I picked up a slice of pizza and took a bite. "We're getting way off track here, girls! Back to business!"

I saw a mischievous look pass between Kelly and Macy as I took a drink of iced tea.

"What about Linda or her mother? Following J.R. to the church office seems pre-meditated and I just don't see her doing that. But, using the letter opener seems like the murderer grabbed whatever was handy, so that could mean it was the result of an argument. Maybe something happened at home before church and she decided to take the opportunity to confront him about it while he was locking up the morning offering. I think Linda stays on the list for now."

Kelly shook her head. "I just cannot believe Linda would ever be able to do anything like this. She was sitting by me in the choir loft the whole time, but when we raised our heads after the prayer, she was gone."

I added a check in both columns.

"I didn't see her mother at church. I suppose she could have followed them there and waited for an oppor-tunity to catch J.R. alone and after the outburst at Linda's this morning, I think her motive could be pretty strong. She didn't hide the fact that she didn't like him at all." Check mark for motive, but question mark for opportunity.

Kelly slipped her laptop out of her black and white houndstooth print computer bag and set it up on the ottoman so we could get comfy while we did some digging.

"Okay, let me show you what I found about the Lindsey's family history." After just a few clicks, Kelly had located the items of interest that she'd found that afternoon at the library. "According to county records, Charles Lindsey and his wife Reba had, at one time, lived in Sweetwater Springs but looks like the Lindseys left the area years ago. They had two daughters, Judith and Elizabeth. Charles was an expert antiques dealer and a well-known author of several books on antiques. I found an old human interest article from The Sweetwater Herald dated June 1970, that says he was known for his extensive travels to research wealthy families across the country for a book he was writing about antique jewelry. It doesn't show any record of Judith marrying but according to the public records her younger sister, Elizabeth, married a man named John Baylor."

Kelly kept scrolling and a link to another old newspaper article, published in August 1989, caught her eye.

"Heavenly days! Look at this one!" Kelly exclaimed. "'*Local Man and Infant Son Disappear*.' This article states that Elizabeth Lindsey Baylor, age 22, died at her home from complications during premature labor and childbirth. Within hours after she was laid to rest in Sweetwater Springs Baptist Church graveyard, her husband and newborn son mysteriously disappeared. It asks that anyone with any information on John please contact the family."

"Does it say if they were ever located?" Macy asked.

"Not in this article. But it looks like a cold case

research article that was written several years later in 2000 says that Charles and Reba searched for their grandchild in the following years until their death, but were never able to find out where John was or if the child survived. It says that Charles and Reba were both buried in the graveyard in Sweetwater Springs alongside Elizabeth. The house and property, which originally had been given to John and Elizabeth, by default then became the property of Judith. I guess it's all been sitting empty for the last forty years. If it's been vacant for that long you know it has to be in bad shape."

"John Baylor." I repeated. "Could this be Sam's father? Is Sam the infant son of John and Elizabeth that disappeared never to be heard from again? If they disappeared in 1989, that would make the baby thirty years old."

"If that's true, then the property would rightfully belong to him at his aunt's death as her last surviving relative." Kelly said.

"Momma and I are going to pay a little visit to Sweetwater Realty tomorrow morning. Maybe I can find out if Sam mentioned anything about this property when he stopped by the realty office."

"Didn't you say that Linda mentioned some property Terrance has his eye on for a condo development? Wouldn't that be a big coincidence if it's all the same property?" Kelly asked.

"How are you going to get him to tell you? I doubt he will volunteer that information. He's probably keeping it close to the vest, so no one else will get the same idea and buy it before he can." Macy chimed in.

"I am only renting this house and I *might* be looking

for a home in the future," I said with a wink. "I'll get him
to print out a list of all the available properties in the area
and we can go from there. Maybe Momma can keep him
talking while I snoop a little."

"Are we still going to the Ladies Club meeting
tomorrow morning?" Macy asked.

Kelly's eyes lit up. "The Sweetwater Springs Ladies
Club? You didn't tell me you were joining!"

"Oh, I forgot to tell you. I ran into Megan Lester at the
Piggly Wiggly last week and she invited Macy and me to
attend the meeting tomorrow. Sounds like it might be a
good way to meet other ladies and maybe volunteer in the
community."

"Plus, it will be a way of meeting other business-
women in town and let everyone know about the bakery."
Macy interjected.

I nodded. "I really want both of us to go! It meets at
the Library at 10:00, right? I think I'll still have plenty of
time to swing by and pick up Momma afterward for our
visit to the realty office."

Macy agreed. "I'll take a change of clothes with me and
you can drop me off at Nana's to change when you pick
her up. I'm sure she'll let me use her Jeep to go back up to
the bakery."

With our plan in the works for Tuesday, Kelly packed
up her laptop and said goodnight as Macy took our plates
and the empty pizza box to the kitchen. She returned with
a small plate of four bite-sized pastries. "I saved one each
of the different macarons I made for the potluck." She
said with a grin. "Which would you like? Chocolate with

chocolate ganache filling, wedding cake, pistachio almond or vanilla rolled in Fruity Pebbles?"

My mouth watered at the descriptions. "Those sound delicious! I hate everyone missed out on them."

"So do I, but Uncle Jake said that everyone at the station has been raving about them."

"I'm sure they'll be knocking down the bakery doors as soon as you open."

"I hope so. I plan to start working on some publicity and marketing stuff next week."

She sat down on the sofa next to me and leaned her head on my shoulder as we both popped a sample in our mouth. "Mom, do you still wonder what really happened to Dad? Do you think we'll ever find out?"

"Of course, I still wonder, Macy. I don't know if I'll ever feel like we have real closure, but that's not always the government's first priority. I have really given all this over to God. I know if the case is going to be resolved, then He'll open a door for that investigation to continue. Until then, I just have to trust that it's time for us to move on with our lives. Does that make sense?"

"Absolutely, Mom. And please don't get upset with me for saying this, but don't you ever get lonely? I know how much you loved Dad and so did I. I'll always miss him, but I just want you to know that when you feel you're ready to meet someone new, it's okay with me."

I hugged her close. "It's almost two years and still I miss him like it was yesterday. He loved us both very much, but I also know that he would not want either of us to mope around for the rest of our lives. He loved living life and he would want us to enjoy it too. God has a plan for whatever comes next for all of us. I am open to whatever that next step is. I'm not going looking for a man, so don't get any ideas about putting me on some dating site, but life is good and I'm ready for the future."

CHAPTER 8

*W*ith Tuesday as a day off, I was back in my favorite spot on the sofa with a light blanket. The mornings were still a little chilly in early May, but it would be hot and muggy by noon. Izzy was curled up in a ball behind my knees. It was cool enough for a nice hot mug of coffee this morning, so I sipped my steaming cup of caffeine while I finished up my morning devotion.

"Whatever you do, work at it with all your heart, as working for the Lord." Colossians 3:23

I loved being back in my hometown and I wanted to make a difference in whatever I decided to get involved in. I prayed that the Ladies' Club would be a place that I could make a contribution to our little town. My thoughts wandered to the murder investigation and I said another prayer for Linda.

I knew the church office would probably be cleared to

reopen tomorrow, so I needed to dig up as much information as I could today. I glanced at the time on my phone and realized I needed to get up and get moving if we were going to make it to the Ladies' Club meeting at the library by ten. I nudged Izzy off my feet and she gave me the side eye and jumped down to curl up on the rug as I headed down the hall to take a quick shower. When I came out of the shower, Izzy had claimed my pillow on the bed to finish her nap.

"What should I wear to meet new friends, Izzy?" I slid the hangers in the closet to the right one by one. "Black jeans and a cute top or my print dress with a jean jacket?" Izzy opened one eye, glaring at me so I took that as a vote to wear the black jeans.

Macy was ready and waiting when I came out of the bedroom.

There wasn't a parking place to be had in front of the library, so I had to park across the street in front of Simm's Hardware. I grabbed my crossbody purse and we trekked across the street and up the sidewalk as quickly as we could, trying to keep the breeze from wrecking my hair. Don't get me wrong, I am always thankful for any breeze that helps cool off the muggy Alabama heat, but I also wanted to make a decent impression on the ladies of Sweetwater Springs. I really wanted both Macy and I to make some good connections for her new business as well as get more involved in the community.

Kelly motioned us to the meeting room down the hall as we entered the library double doors.

"Don't you all look spiffy today!" she smiled as we rushed past her desk. I smiled a big smile, took a deep breath, tucked my crazy hair behind my ears and walked in.

Immediately, I was hit with a barrage of welcomes and hugs and how's your "momma'nem", a term that I had used all my life. I never realized until we moved to Texas that people outside of Alabama don't really have any idea what you're saying.

After a lot of social pleasantries, Megan called the meeting to order. Megan Lester spoke with the classic southern drawl. Just like you hear in the movies. She reminded me of Lou Ann Poovey, Gomer Pyle's girlfriend on the TV show I watched growing up. She dropped her "r's" off the end of many words and talked slowly and deliberately, dragging out each word like honey dripping from a honeycomb. I wasn't sure if it was all put on or if she was the real thing.

The first thing she did was welcome everyone and introduce me and Macy to the rest of the club.

"Good mornin', ladies! We have two guests today! You all know Annie *Milla*, retired math *teacha* from our little ol' town. Well, this is her *daw-tah*, Glory *Haa-pah*. Glory grew up here and many of you may know her as well. This is her *daw-tah*, Macy *Haa-pah* who has just finished her *masta's* degree and is moving here also." They are gonna tell us a little about themselves."

Of course, many of them knew me as Annie's daughter or remembered me from high school years ago, but most of them had never met Macy. She told them about her vision for the bakery and coffee shop and everyone seemed ecstatic at the idea of her plans for the old furniture store.

There were several items on the agenda for discussion today, like an upcoming purse auction to raise money for new elementary school playground equipment. Now, I'd never heard of a purse auction, but evidently, ladies all over town donated purses in excellent condition to be bid on in a silent auction. I had several in my closet at home that I could donate. To a southern girl, a purse is a necessity for each outfit. You can never have too many, so why not have all that money you were going to spend anyway, go to a great cause?

The project that really grabbed my attention was the Fall Harvest Festival. I know it's only May, but the group was going all out this year and planning two big town celebrations back to back. The Harvest Festival in November and Christmas Snowflake Celebration in December. Of course, it was a rare sight to have snowflakes in Alabama before February, if then, but the name conjured up dreams of a white Christmas even though we rarely saw one.

As if my hand had a mind of its own, it automatically raised when Megan asked for a volunteer to organize the Harvest Festival and I also volunteered to serve on a committee for the Christmas event and somehow got roped into organizing the annual purse auction in September as well. I don't know what I was thinking, but I guess I figured I would just jump in with both feet. I hoped I didn't regret it.

After Megan covered the past business, the current business, and the future business, we finally got around to the good part; the food and socializing. After filling our plates with assorted goodies, Macy talked with a group of the younger women and I joined Megan as she introduced me to a group of ladies she was deep in discussion with.

"Glory, this is Susan Duvall and Mary Ellen Simms. Susan is the assistant to the *May-ah* and Mary Ellen's husband, Frank, owns the *hardway-ah sto-ah* across Main Street. Ladies, this is Glory. She is the church secretary at the Baptist church."

"So nice to meet you ladies!" I smiled, noticing freshly manicured nails and an overwhelming scent of cottonwood.

"We were just discussing the rumor of a condominium project on Smith Lake. Have you heard anything down at the church about it?" Mary Ellen feigned a smile as she sipped her tea.

"I didn't hear it at the church, but I have heard about town that Terrance Wolfe is looking for property to do something like that. He had been trying to get J.R. Jenkins on board with it but, of course, that deal may be dead in the water now."

They all raised an eyebrow at my choice of words. "Sorry, I guess that came out wrong." I winced.

They all three nodded with a knowing glance at each other. Their facial expressions were so non-committal, I couldn't tell if they would be for or against such a development.

"Do you think the people of the town would be in support of a condo development? I mean, just think of all the revenue it could bring in to revitalize this beautiful downtown area."

Mary Ellen was the first to speak up. "I know Frank and I would support it and I believe most of the downtown merchants would as well, but I think the opposition would come from those who own property on the lake. Especially those that live in close proximity to the land that would be developed."

"I can't speak for the Mayor's office, but I do believe he will hear all sides before the zoning committee votes to allow the development. That is, if and when it's proposed." Susan said.

Megan nodded in agreement. "I think *Mista* Wolfe should be really careful who he *sha-ahs* his plans with. The more it spreads all *ovah* town, the more certain people could get all worked up. I would hate for things to get ugly before there's even a real proposal on the table."

"Do you think there's a chance it could get that bad?" I raised my eyebrows.

"Oh, I definitely do. There are property *land-ownahs* who have fortunes sunk into their lake properties and they won't sit idly by and let anything happen to lessen their property values. *Mista* Wolfe had *bettah* watch his back."

Did that sound like a veiled threat with syrup dripping from it, or was I just reading too much into her reaction? Could someone have gotten wind of the condo talk and made sure that J.R. never had the chance to support Terrance in the project? If Terrance pursues the project, would certain property owners be upset enough to do whatever it takes to stop it from moving forward and come after him too?

I nodded and made my way around to the other clusters of ladies, saying hello to those I knew and meeting lots of new friends. This was going to be a fun group.

Sure, there were a few stick-in-the-muds who were a little too hoity-toity for their designer britches, but overall, I knew I was going to enjoy spending some time with these ladies. And as Granny used to say . . . "a good time was had by all."

Macy and I stopped by Kelly's desk on our way out. "I hate you had to miss the meeting. It was really fun. Sounds like they have several worthwhile projects on the agenda. I'm excited to help!"

Macy snickered, "I think they saw fresh blood with Mom and took advantage of her inability to say no."

She shrugged, "I can almost guarantee that's what happened. It's like they have a pushover radar or something." Kelly laughed and I shot her a pointed glare. "I always hate when I have to miss it. I'll let you fill me in later on all the projects *and* the gossip!" She winked.

"I'm headed now to pick up Momma and drop off Macy. I'll let you know how our visit with Terrance and Jeannie goes. I do have one quick question. Do you have any idea where Megan Lester lives?"

"Sure, she and her husband have a huge house out on the lake!"

Momma was rocking in the rocker on her front porch, drinking her second cup of coffee of the morning when I pulled the Honda in behind her red Jeep. "Mornin' Glory! Mornin' Macy! How was your meeting?" she sang as we bounced up the porch steps.

"Mornin' Momma! It was really nice! I think I'm gonna enjoy getting to know that group of ladies. Are you ready for some sleuthing today? I've got some ideas on who's next on our list. Let me grab a glass of tea and I'll come fill you in." I breezed past her and headed to the kitchen. I could always count on her to have plenty of sweet tea on hand.

"Macy, are you joining us today?" Momma asked.

"No, I went to the meeting with Mom, but I need to go do some work at the bakery. I brought a change of clothes. Do you mind if I use your Jeep to go back to town? After we're done, Mom can drop you there to pick it up and I can ride home with her."

"That's fine with me! I'll leave my keys on the table by the front door," Momma agreed.

Sitting down in the swing, I pushed myself one good time to get it started. "After Kelly left last night, I texted Jake just to see if I could weasel any info out of him. He said that Terrance Wolfe says he was nowhere near the church Sunday, but there's nobody to verify his alibi. We need to see if Jeannie, at the realty office, can give us any idea about where he was. Wait till you hear what we discovered last night about the Lindsays!"

* * *

It was almost noon and Main Street was getting busy, but I spotted a parking place in front of Sweetwater Springs Realty and pulled in.

"Good morning, ladies! How can I help y'all today?" the lady, and I use the term loosely, behind the desk drawled as we walked in. "My name is Jeannie. Are you looking for a new home in our little town?" She smacked and popped her gum with gusto as she got up out of her chair to greet us. Her dyed orange hair was piled up on top of her head in a beehive that tilted to one side as she leaned over the desk to shake my hand. A wide belt separating her tight pencil skirt from the low-cut blouse, was cinched so tight I thought the girls were going to pop right out. The office reeked of cigarettes. I wasn't sure if she was a smoker or if it was Terrance. I didn't think J.R. smoked, but who knows. There seemed to be a lot of things about J.R. I didn't know.

"Good morning, Jeannie," Momma said. "My name is Annie Miller and this is my daughter, Glory. She just moved back here from Texas."

"Well, I sure am happy to meet you!" Jeannie gushed with a big smile full of surprisingly white teeth. "Are you looking for a new home?"

"I'm renting right now and it's possible that I might be interested in the near future. I'm just really on a little fact-finding mission today. You know . . . just to see what's available in my price range."

I gave Jeannie a quick rundown of preferences in home location and price range. "If you ladies will have a seat, I'll see what I can pull up on the computer and we'll take a look!" Jeannie pointed toward a nice leather sofa and seating area with real estate magazines strewn strategically around the table.

"Do you mind if I use your ladies' room?" I asked.

"Not at all. Just down the hall past the office on the right." She nodded in the direction of what must be Terrance's and J.R.'s offices.

I casually walked down the hall until I was sure I was well out of sight. The door to the left was cracked open a bit. Terrance Wolfe's name was on the nameplate affixed to it. The light was off, so I inched the door open just a little. Looking around as fast as I could, I noticed a laptop on the desk. Carefully opening it, I squiggled the mouse on the desk to wake up the sleep mode. I clicked on his browsing history and blinked my eyes a couple of times to focus. He had been reading some of the same articles that Kelly found about the Lindsey family. It certainly seemed like he had quite an interest in that property. Quickly, I closed the laptop, stepped into the ladies' room and flushed the toilet.

CHAPTER 9

"Glory, I'm sorry, but I haven't been able to find one home that meets the criteria you gave me. If you will give me your contact information, I'll have Terrance give you a call if anything comes on the market that you might be interested in."

"I would appreciate that," I smiled. "I was so sorry to hear about J.R. I know it must have been such a shock. Had you worked with him long?"

"Yes, it's so sad. I've worked here since the day the office opened two years ago. I love working here." Jeannie seemed like she might be willing to talk, so I decided to bait her with a few more questions.

"That's so nice. It sure makes a big difference when you love what you do! Has it been awkward lately? I heard things had gotten a little tense between J.R. and Terrance. A friend told me she overheard them arguing recently." I prodded, hoping I wasn't pushing my luck too far with more questions.

"Well . . ." Jeannie glanced around like she was making sure that no one else could hear and she continued. "Terrance has big dreams for this business," she had such a dreamy look in her eyes, I wouldn't have been surprised if big red hearts replaced her pupils. "J.R was always dragging his feet about moving forward. He just wouldn't even listen to or consider any of Terrance's amazing ideas! He was so hateful. It was always his way or the highway." She said without even taking a breath.

"I get the feeling that you weren't a member of the J.R fan club, then?"

"No, ma'am, I wasn't. I didn't like working with the guy, but I surely didn't want to see him dead, if that's what you're implying!"

"Oh no, certainly not! What about Terrance, though. Is he concerned that the police are looking at him as a suspect? I mean, he did have a lot to gain with J.R. out of the way," I pushed for a little more information.

"There is no way Terrance had anything to do with it. We were out on his boat Sunday . . ." Her eyes got wide and her hand flew to her mouth.

"You were with Terrance Sunday?"

"Well . . . uh . . . we haven't really told anyone that we've been dating. Terrance doesn't think it looks professional. But yes, I met him out there around 12:30. We had a late lunch and lazed around on the boat for the rest of the day."

"That sounds like a nice, relaxing afternoon." Momma commented.

"Yes, Terrance has been so stressed out over that old

woman that keeps pushing him to sell her dilapidated old property."

"Really? Who is that?" I gave Momma the side eye.

"Some lady named Judith Lindsey. She's all kinds of crazy. Called him every single day for a month to see if it's sold yet."

I raised an eyebrow and glanced at Momma. "Hmmm . . . sounds like a crazy one alright. So where is the property? Is it not in a good area? Is that why it hasn't sold yet?" I needed an address or at least a general direction to that house.

"No, it's ten acres of prime lakefront in the Upper End on Edgewater Road, but the house is in terrible condition and she's asking way too much for it." Jeannie's eyes lit up. "Just between us, I think Terrance would love to have it. He says it's a perfect location for the vacation rental condo project that he's been wanting to build."

The Upper End was how the locals referred to the north end of Smith Lake. It's where the majority of the bigger estates and lake homes were situated right on the water with private boat docks and gated communities. The commercial enterprises, like the Lake House Café, Lakeside Motel, boat docks, bait shops, jet ski rentals and other businesses seemed to stay mostly on the other end of the lake.

"Why doesn't he just buy it from her?" I asked.

"Oh, it's way out of his price range. He's been trying to get her to drop the price, but so far, she won't budge." She was on a roll. "That old lady hasn't even seen the property in forty years. She has no idea the shape it's in."

"Doesn't Judith have any other family that would want

the property?" I could see a big motive forming in my head.

"No, I think she's the last one left in her family. She says since she has no one to leave it to in her will, she might as well sell everything off and enjoy spending all her money." Jeannie shrugged. "The funniest thing, though. A couple weeks ago, the calls just totally stopped. Terrance got spooked that maybe she was changing her mind and he called to convince her to come see the property, thinking if she sees it in person, she might come down on the price. She's supposed to get into town about two o'clock Thursday afternoon. He's planning to pick her up at the motel shortly after and drive her out to the property."

Nodding to Momma that it was time to go, I got up. "Well, we've taken up enough of your time. Again, I'm sorry about J.R., but I wish you and Terrance the best in moving forward in the business."

"And in your relationship!" Momma winked at Jeannie with a big smile as they walked out the door.

"What would you think about taking a drive down Edgewater Road to see if we can find that property?" I suggested.

"We'll have to be careful. I don't want Terrance to catch us snooping around the house." Momma said.

About a mile after we turned onto Edgewater Road, we saw a Sweetwater Springs Realty sign in the yard. "That must be it." I said pointing. "It really is run down. I was expecting a newer house than this one. Maybe I just assumed the Lindseys built this house in the 70's, but it's much older than that."

Momma shrugged, "Looks to me like it could be about 100 years old."

As we drove up the long, gravel driveway shaded by huge poplar trees and stopped in front of the house, we could see that the porch sagged and the roof needed replacing. We walked up the front steps, the boards creaking with each step like the next one would give way. Sitting empty for so many years, it really showed it. I grasped the doorknob fully expecting it to be locked up tight, but it turned with ease and squeaked as it slowly swung open. I guess it was in such bad condition, Terrance didn't think it would matter if it was locked or not. We entered the door into a formal entryway. Faded floral wallpaper hung haphazardly peeling off the walls. As we walked through each room of the house, stopping to notice the dusty, faded portraits of family members on many of the walls, all that was jumping out at me was the fact the whole place needed a gut job and total remodel. Of course, if Terrance wanted to build a condo development here, the house would be torn down anyway. I'm sure that he was hoping that once Judith sees the house, he can use its condition to his advantage to talk down the price. What really caught my eye was that in almost every room, furniture still sat covered with bedsheets. Antiques were everywhere. Some of this stuff might be worth a lot of money, which really made me wonder why it wasn't locked when we arrived. Momma walked down the hall as I checked out the kitchen.

"Glory! Come in here! I'm in the back bedroom."

I made my way down the hall following the sound of her voice. Scanning what must have been the master bedroom, she pointed to some loose floorboards buckled up in the corner. I knelt down to take a closer look and realized that I could see right through to the dirt underneath the house. Something caught my eye. There was something white showing through one of the holes in the floor. I tugged on one of the floorboards and on closer inspection, saw what appeared to be a piece of fabric. As we pulled the board away far enough to reach in between the boards, I carefully pulled out what looked like a ladies' dress rolled up and tied with a string. White cotton with tiny little yellow flowers sprinkled throughout. I untied the string and unrolled the fabric. Momma's eyes got as big as saucers and I heard her gasp. Jewelry. And not the fake stuff, but a beautiful necklace with a large emerald the size of a quarter as the centerpiece, surrounded by diamonds with smaller emeralds on either side.

We both froze, our mouths gaped open.

"Holy smokes!! That looks real! Why on earth do you think it would be hidden there?"

"I have no idea, but we certainly have another interesting piece to this puzzle."

I took my phone from my pocket and snapped a quick picture of the necklace. Something about it looked familiar. I knew I had seen that necklace somewhere before. But where? I retraced my steps back through the house, wracking my brain and there it was. The portrait of a young woman wearing the necklace. The inscription underneath the picture read, "Elizabeth Ruth Lindsey".

"Shouldn't we call Jake?" Momma asked.

"You know he would have a fit if he finds out we broke into a house!" I shook my head. "Technically, the front door wasn't locked, so it wasn't breaking --- just entering. I wonder if Terrance knows about this. Could that be another reason he wants this property so badly?" I ran back to the bedroom and quickly laid the necklace back in the fabric and rolled it back up, placing it back under the floorboard. Yes, this is definitely something I was keeping to myself until I could find out more.

"I'm getting hungry. Why don't we stop by the Lake House Café and grab a bite for lunch since we're out this way." Momma suggested.

As if on cue, my stomach let out a growl and I realized the couple of little tea sandwiches I had at the meeting were long gone. I glanced down at my watch and realized it was almost one o'clock. "Sounds good. I'm starved."

We waved at the waitress and slid into an empty booth in the back of the café so we could have a little privacy. It was a beautiful day in May and the boating season was just heating up. I cringed at the sound of the old metal chairs scooting across the faded green, linoleum floor. This place was full of memories for me. It hadn't changed much since my high school years. It had been a regular hangout for a generation of teenagers. That group included me, Dave, Jake and Kelly. I knew the first time I laid eyes on Dave that he was the guy I would marry. Sure, we'd had some on again, off again times throughout high school, like the time I went out with Jimmy Steele just to spite him or when he took my cousin to the Homecoming Dance and I cried for a week. But deep down, we both always knew we were meant to be together. I looked across the room and envisioned myself at sixteen shooting pool with friends or sharing a burger and fries in the corner booth with Dave. Of course, we both had much more hair in the seventies. I was channeling my inner Farrah Fawcett with flybacks, long since chopped off in favor of practicality, and Dave looked like a rock star with a head full of wavy locks. At least that's the way I remembered us.

The Lake House Café was separated into two areas; one large room, open and airy with floor to ceiling windows on three walls. A deck surrounded the outside and all of it overlooked Smith Lake. The second room off to the right was called Golddiggers Bar and Grill. It was open later hours and offered more "night life"; if there was such a thing in Sweetwater Springs. It was early in the season, but by the time school was out for the summer, the café would be packed at lunchtime. It was a little bit of a drive out of town but always worth the drive and the wait.

"Afternoon ladies!" the waitress said as she glanced up at the clock. "What can I get you today?"

"Are we too late for the lunch special?" Momma asked.

"No ma'am. We're still serving lunch."

"Perfect! I'll have the lunch special, pot roast with vegetables, mashed potatoes with brown gravy, green beans, a roll and a big glass of sweet tea!" Momma spouted off the menu like she worked there.

"Oohhhh, I'll have the same! Except I think I'd rather have fried okra instead of the green beans and sweet tea for me, also." I could taste it already.

It was late enough that we had missed the lunch rush, so I wondered if the waitress might sit a minute and tell us anything she's heard or seen that could help us out. I glanced up at her name tag.

"Jolene, could you take a little break and sit for a minute? We have a couple of questions we'd like to ask you."

"Sure, I guess so. Let me go put your orders in and I'll be right back with your drinks."

In a few minutes, she was back with our drinks and pulled up an empty chair to the end of our booth table.

"I heard you've been asking questions around town about J.R.'s death. Does that have anything to do with what you want to ask me?"

"Yes, I know that Terrance was seen and heard down here making some unfriendly comments about J.R. and several people I've talked to have verified that they heard similar things."

"Yeah, he seemed to be really upset that J.R. didn't want to expand into rentals. He seemed bound and determined to find a way to go ahead with that condo project. Of course, he was falling down drunk when he said all of it, so you never can tell if he meant any of it or not."

"What about a guy named Sam Baylor? He's an old friend of J.R. and Linda's and we think he might be staying at the motel."

"I know who you're talking about. He has been here a couple of times to eat."

"Did you ever see him with J.R. or Terrance?

"No, but late Saturday night . . . had to have been close to eleven, he was in here with Chris Lester."

"Chris Lester as in Megan Lester's husband? They own property on the lake?"

"Yeah. I served them a few rounds of drinks and from what little I overheard, I gathered that Chris was trying to talk Sam into selling some property to him."

"Did you hear what Sam said? Did he agree to anything?"

"All I heard was that he didn't really own the property yet, but when he did, it would go to the highest bidder. "Your food is up in the window, so I need to get back to work." Jolene got up and replaced the chair at the nearby table.

"Thanks, Jolene." I said as she disappeared into the kitchen.

I leaned across the table toward Momma. "I think we need to talk to Sam Baylor. Remember, I saw him sitting with J.R. Sunday morning for a short time, but he got up and slipped out just before J.R. got up to help with the offering. I don't recall ever seeing him come back in for the close of the service."

Momma nodded in agreement. "That places him at the scene with an opportunity to commit the crime and we already know he has a motive."

"Now we know that getting rid of J.R. not only gets him Linda, but it also keeps the bidding going on the property he will eventually own. Without J.R. to block Terrance's project, it could be an all out bidding war between Terrance and Chris Lester. And I'll bet Chris is willing to pay a pretty penny to keep that condo project from going in." Momma said.

"I think our next move should be to swing by the

Lakeside Motel and see what we can find out. It's the only motel in town and if Jolene has seen Sam several times, you know he's probably got a room there."

Jolene delivered our lunches, so we dug in while we came up with a plan for visiting the motel.

CHAPTER 10

The Lakeside Motel was a short drive. It was a small, family-owned motel that stretched along the water just around the bend from the café. There were about thirty rooms in the motel that was built with brick, now painted gray. It was older, but very well-kept and updated thanks to the Johnson family who had owned it for as long as I could remember.

Josie Johnson was at the front desk when we walked in. Josie was a member of Sweetwater Springs Baptist also and served on several committees with Momma.

"Annie! Glory! What brings you two ladies out this way?" she greeted us with a sweet smile.

"We are following up on a visitor from church on Sunday." I fudged. "I think his name is Sam Baylor. Is he staying here at the motel? We'd love to pay him a quick visit." I really felt bad misleading Josie, but, after all, I am a member of the church staff and we did need to meet all the guests that visited our services, right?

"Yes, I believe Mr. Baylor is staying in Room 11. It's

down at the far end on the back side. I'm not sure if he's here right now, but you are welcome to go knock and see. If you want to leave him a message, just let me know and I'll make sure he gets it!"

"Thanks, Josie!" We chimed in unison as we walked back to the car. Driving down to the end of the building, I pulled around the corner to the back side of the motel. These rooms overlooked a beautiful view of Smith Lake and the best part was that Josie wouldn't have a direct view of us while we did our looking around.

Each motel room had a parking space with a coordinating room number stenciled on the pavement. Space number 11 was empty.

I knocked, just to be sure, but there was no answer. I tried the doorknob, but as I expected, it was locked.

"Let's try there!" Momma nudged me a little harder than she intended and I stumbled over a crack in the parking lot. "Sorry!" She grinned and pointed to a small screened porch just off the back of the room.

"Shhhhh!" I motioned for Momma to follow tiptoeing gingerly around to the deck. The door to the screened porch was unlocked. "A lot of people don't think about checking the sliding doors to their patio before they go out. Maybe the door to the room off the deck isn't locked either!" I whispered and smiled as I felt the sliding door glide open.

The room was pretty basic but clean and looked like it would provide the necessities. The carpet looked fairly new in a nice neutral light brown coordinating with the brown and blue floral bedspread on the double bed. Hanging over the bed was a beautiful painting of a lake scene done by a local artist that Kelly had mentioned when we were out shopping last weekend. I made a mental note to Google him to see more of his work.

"Look for anything that ties him to J.R. and Linda or anything concerning the property on Edgewater Road. We need to do this quickly because we don't know when he'll be coming back."

Looking in all the hiding places I had seen my favorite TV sleuths find things, I searched the bedroom while Momma skimmed the bathroom. I looked in the night-stand drawer, behind the mirror over the dresser and even glanced through the pockets of a duffle bag. All clean as a whistle. I lifted the corner of the mattress and bingo! A large manila envelope. Carefully, I dumped all the contents onto the bed.

"Here are some old photos, a birth certificate and a small envelope of some kind."

The birth certificate read Samuel John Baylor. Born: July 29, 1988; Parents: John Joseph Baylor and Elizabeth Lindsey Baylor.

The two photos were of a young man and woman. The first one looked to be at their wedding. The other was of the same couple but the woman was obviously expecting a child. Writing on the back of each photo said simply: John and Lizzie.

Momma picked up the small envelope reading the single name written across the front; Sam.

She carefully unfolded the letter inside and began to read:

My dearest son,

I don't have long left in this world and there are things you need to know. Things I should have told you long ago. Many years ago, your grandfather came into possession of a very valuable piece of jewelry on his travels researching antiques. He gave it to your mother on the occasion of her 20th birthday. It was a beautiful emerald necklace and it was her most beloved possession.

After we were married, I began gambling with the men at work and pretty soon was in over my head. I feared for my life because of the debts I owed to the wrong people. I planned to secretly take the necklace and sell it to get money to pay my debts. Your mother saw me taking it and we fought as she tried to take it from me. She was 8 months pregnant with you at the time. She tripped and fell causing her to go into early labor. As the doctor was attending to her, I took the necklace and wrapped it in one of her dresses and put it away in a drawer.

She never regained consciousness. Somehow the doctor was able to save you, but I lost her.

As soon as the funeral was over, I went to the house and took the dress and necklace from the drawer and hid it under a loose board in our bedroom floor, planning to come back for it later. Then I took you and left. I knew I could never live with myself in that house knowing what I had done and you were all I had left of her. I took you to my sister, Mary Baylor and she agreed to help me raise you. A week later, I was arrested and convicted of robbery and sent to prison. Mary raised you as her own and never told a soul.

I'm sure your grandparents have passed on, but your mother had a sister named Judith Lindsey. She had no children, so you are the last living heir to the Lindsey fortune. Find Judith and

show her this letter to prove who you are. That property and the
necklace with it are rightfully yours. You deserve it.
I hope that someday you can find it in your heart to forgive me.
Goodbye, son.
Your father, John Baylor

"Oh my goodness! That is unbelievable!" I was speechless.

Quickly, I snapped pictures of all the items then carefully put everything back into the envelope and placed it back under the mattress. Taking one last look around the room, I noticed a Lakeside Motel logo notepad by the phone with something scribbled on it.

"*925 Honeysuckle Rd.* . . . isn't that J.R. and Linda's address? And look at this . . ." I continued, "*Matthew* ~~*Jenkins*~~ *Baylor*? What could that mean? Isn't that Linda's son's name. . . Matthew?"

"Oh no. You don't think . . ." Momma stopped midsentence.

"Yes, that's exactly what I think." I finished Momma's thoughts. "Matthew isn't J.R.'s son. His real father is Sam Baylor. That's what Brigette was hinting at when she told me about the one-night stand between Sam and Linda before the wedding. He's still secretly in love with Linda and came back to try to convince her to leave J.R. so they could be together. I wonder if he knew he had a son, or if this is new information.

"Either way, it's a whopper of a motive if I've ever heard one."

We sneaked back out the way we came in and I pulled out of the parking lot as inconspicuously as I could.

"I think we've had enough investigating for one day.

Let's go home and we can try to put some of these puzzle pieces together."

We drove straight to the bakery to pick up Momma's Jeep and Macy, but the Jeep wasn't there, so we went on to Momma's to find Macy swinging on the front porch. I poured all three of us a glass of sweet tea and I sat down on the swing with Macy and Momma sat in her favorite rocking chair.

"So tell me what you found out!" Macy said, rubbing the palms of her hands together excitedly.

I pulled out my trusty notepad. "Okay, here's what we know so far: Linda was being abused by J.R. and they were in financial trouble. As much as I hate to say it, I still think she stays on the list. I'm not sure she had opportunity. But Kelly did say that when she opened her eyes after the prayer, Linda was gone. She could have followed J.R. to the office to drop off the money. She knew the routine."

"Linda's mom, Connie, knew all about the way J.R. treated Linda and Matthew." Momma continued. "And mothers will do anything to protect their children and grandchildren, so I think Connie is a valid suspect."

"Even though we didn't see her at church, doesn't mean she wasn't there waiting to get J.R. alone." I frowned at my own far-fetched scenario. "It isn't probable, but it is possible, so I don't think we can mark Connie off the suspect list just yet."

"Now, we get to Sam. He has to be our number one suspect right now. The motives just keep adding up for him. If he's been pining away for Linda for the last 3 years and if he just found out he has a son he didn't know about, that may have sent him over the edge." I reasoned.

Momma nodded in agreement. "Yes, he's definitely got the biggest motive right now and he had opportunity because he was seen at church. You saw him slip out at about the time J.R. took up the offering. He could definitely have been waiting on his chance to confront him."

"Wait! What?" Macy exclaimed. "What son?"

I pulled up the pictures I had taken with my phone in the motel room of the letter from Sam's father as well as the note I'd found beside the phone and showed them to Macy.

"Wow. That's incredible!" Macy gave another big push in the swing.

I looked at the last name on the list. "What about Terrance? We know J.R. was trying to block him on the condo project and didn't want to expand the business. We know he wants that Lindsey property to use for the condo project. If he knows about that necklace, that would make him even more desperate to get rid of J.R. and figure out a way to get that property.

"And don't forget about all those antiques. They could be worth a fortune." Momma reminded me.

"I know Jeannie said she was with him, but what if they are in it together and she's just covering for him?"

"Do we need to add Chris Lester to the suspect list? If he thought Terrance needed J.R. to be able to buy the property, maybe he or someone else associated with the lake landowners got rid of him."

"But why not just take out Terrance? Why, J.R.?" asked Macy.

"True, unless it was the result of an argument and it wasn't premeditated. Maybe Chris or another landowner took the opportunity to confront J.R. about the deal and they got into a heated argument that went too far. The use of my letter opener instead of a knife still suggests to me that it might not have been premeditated."

"Since Chief Detective Walker confirmed that the bank bag was still missing, I think the robbery scenario needs to stay on the list." Momma said.

Swinging back and forth in the breeze, I tried to relax, but my brain was still barreling full speed ahead. There's no way I would be able to stop the runaway freight train in my head until this murderer was behind bars.

"Jake and Kelly are coming over for dinner tonight. I will see if I can wheedle a little information out of Jake. I know he's not technically assigned to the case, but maybe I can get him to spill a little about what they've discovered." I decided.

"Are you going to share all our information with him?"

"I don't want to jump the gun and put him on the trail of an innocent person. I think we need to get a little more information first." Setting my tea glass in the sink, I gathered my things to go.

Momma had followed me into the kitchen. "I think that's probably best. I wouldn't want to embarrass Linda for no reason. But just remember, if it starts looking dangerous, we go straight to Jake."

"Yes, Ma'am!" I nodded with a little mock salute. "I'll talk to you tomorrow and let you know what I find out from Jake."

"And I'll let you know if I hear any good gossip at Rummy Club tonight. I'm making that Blueberry Cream

Cheese Dip Mix I bought yesterday at Busy Bee. It goes perfect with animal crackers!"

"Oh, that reminds me, can I borrow your bundt pan? I have been wanting to try a bundt cake and I keep forgetting to ask you!"

"Of course, honey! I'll get it back the next time I'm over. I don't use it that often. What kind are you thinking about baking?"

"I think I'll just start with something simple like a butter cake with lemon icing drizzle. Macy can teach me some baking basics!"

"I think that's a great place to start! Let me know how it turns out!"

With bundt pan in hand, we headed home.

CHAPTER 11

*A*fter taking Izzy out for a quick walk, I plugged in my almost dead phone and selected the music app and connected to the Bluetooth speakers Macy had just given me for my birthday last month. I exhaled a long deep breath. Just the smooth crooning melodies of the Rat Pack put me in a much better frame of mind. As Dean Martin glided over the melody of "Everybody Loves Somebody Sometime", I began to assemble the ingredients for all my recipes and started to work preparing supper. Tonight's menu was going to be Hodge Podge soup, Mexican cornbread (Momma's recipe), tossed salad and Lemon Butter Bundt cake. Hodge Podge soup was quick and easy. Except for the little time it took to brown and drain the ground beef, the rest was just combining different cans of soup and a few seasonings. Easy peasy. It would probably be one of the last times I fixed soup until the fall. In May it was still cooling off when the sun went down, but before long, it would be hotter than Satan's housecat at night.

With the soup on the stove, I preheated the oven and pulling out Momma's recipe card she had written out for me, I mixed up the Mexican cornbread and slid the iron skillet in the hot oven.

Since I had finally remembered to borrow that bundt pan from Momma, I was excited to try it out. I decided on a simple butter cake with lemon glaze for my first attempt.

Macy went into baking class mode and walked me through mixing the cake. After a lot of laughing and more than a little mess, we got it in the oven. Thankfully, it cooked at the same oven temperature as the cornbread so all I had left to do was the salad and dinner would be ready.

I scooped Izzy's food and she immediately started tap dancing around her bowl. She scarfed down her food and looked up at me with sweet eyes hiding behind those long bushy eyebrows.

"Miss Priss, if you think you are getting extra, you are sadly mistaken. We've got to watch your girlish figure! Maybe a treat later if you're a good girl."

As if she understood completely, she bopped off into the living room to curl up on the rug with her stuffed toy, happy as a clam.

Jake and Kelly arrived and came in sniffing the air. "Woman, you got this house 'stankin' like food!" Jake announced in his best good-ole-boy voice. He died laughing at his own humor, which had all of us laughing with him.

Kelly lifted the lid to the soup and took a whiff. "This is some good stuff! I have missed your Hodge Podge soup!

Your momma used to make it for us all the time when I would sleep over at your house! Can I do anything to help?"

"If you want to put ice in the glasses while I throw the salad together, that would be great." I said checking on the cornbread and dessert. Both were just perfect.

In an effort to make it sound like small talk, I thought I might as well jump right in. "So Jake, how's the investigation coming? Got any suspects?"

Jake gave me the side eye and grinned. He recognized my tactics but I guess he figured it wouldn't hurt to give me a little information. Probably thinking it would keep me from playing detective on my own.

"I can tell you that the coroner determined that your letter opener was definitely the murder weapon."

"Ugh," I groaned. "That really stinks. I don't know If I'll ever be able to use it again without thinking about all this. Since it was a gift from Pastor Dan, I hate to get rid of it."

"There were no fingerprints on it. Not even yours. It had been wiped clean. And the body was moved. He was killed in your office."

"Oh no, I was afraid of that. How am I gonna go back in there and work knowing all this happened right there?" I moaned. "At least I'm not a suspect any longer, though, right, Jake?"

"I suppose you're in the clear. Hunt reinstated me to start actively working the case again." Jake continued, "We brought Terrance Wolfe in for questioning, but we didn't really have enough to hold him. He and J.R. had been seen in a very public, heated argument recently. But arguing isn't a crime or the proof of one." Not really new information. The ladies at Bonnie's Cut and Curl had beat him to the punch on that one, but I decided not to bring that to his attention.

"He swears he was out on his boat alone, drinking beer Sunday morning. But with no one to corroborate his alibi, we can't be sure."

I hesitated, debating if I should tell him about Jeannie and Terrance.

I was about to tell him what Jeannie has said, when Kelly asked, "How about J.R.'s wife? Does she know anything helpful?"

"I don't know. Glory, why don't you tell us what you think? I hear you and Momma made a nice little, Christian visit to Linda yesterday." Jake said not even looking up from his soup.

Macy looked at me wide-eyed, waiting to see how I was going to get out of this one.

"I asked you to stay out of things that don't concern you, Glory." Jake continued.

"But, technically, anything that involves the church and my office concerns me." I looked up at Jake sheepishly.

Kelly's gaze was moving back and forth like she was watching a tennis match, grinning from ear to ear. She was enjoying this.

"Well, I actually did get some helpful information that I was planning to pass on to you. I just didn't want to embarrass Linda unnecessarily." I glared at Jake.

"If you're talking about the fact that they were flat broke and he was abusive, we already knew that. Her mother called in a report about two months ago, but Linda refused to press charges, so there was nothing we could do." Jake shook his head.

"So, do you consider Linda or her mother a valid suspect?" I speculated. "Linda was at church for sure. I didn't see her mom, but I figured it would be easy enough for her to follow them to church and wait to find an opportunity to whack J.R. You know a momma will do just about anything to protect her children . . . or grand-children."

"Her mother was at her own church for the service there. Plenty of Methodists saw her, so she's in the clear." Jake looked amused that so far, he had busted my suspect list wide open.

"Tell me all about the Ladies' Club meeting this morn-ing!" Kelly suggested feeling the need to change the subject.

Thankful for the opportunity to turn off the heat that I felt rising in the room, I dove into that conversation head on. "We really enjoyed it! They have several worthwhile service projects coming up and I was really excited to hear about some events in the fall that will be a lot of fun and bring in visitors to the town, especially during the lake off-season."

Macy jumped into the conversation. "I'm really excited too! I hope I have the shop up and running by then! I can't wait to decorate my beautiful picture windows for all the holidays!" she beamed.

"They are going all out this year with a Harvest Festival in November and a Christmas Snowflake Cele-bration in December. There will be vendor booths for crafts and food as well as games and activities for the kids!"

"Wow! That sounds like a huge undertaking! Are you going to try to help out with any of them?" Kelly asked.

I gave a sheepish side glance. "I may or may not have volunteered to head up the Fall Harvest Festival."

"So, Megan Lester roped you in from the get-go, huh?" Kelly laughed.

"Well, on the bright side, I only volunteered to assist with the other event! And Macy and I can tag team!" I laughed.

"Absolutely!" Macy nodded just as her phone vibrated a call. She glanced down to check the caller.

"Can y'all excuse me for a minute? I'll be right back!" She said jumping up from the table and scurrying down the hall to her room.

"I wonder who that was. Did you see the smile on her face when she saw the caller ID?" Kelly eased up from the table and inched her way about halfway down the hall.

"What in the world are you doing? Get back in here before she catches you trying to eavesdrop!" I said in a hushed tone motioning her back to the table.

"I just wanted to do a little intel. You are trying so hard to stay out of her business and somebody has to find out the juicy stuff!" Kelly laughed. "Haven't you noticed the stupid grin on her face lately?"

"No, I guess I've been so wrapped up in all the crazy things going on, I haven't noticed." I silently kicked myself for letting all this take over my life to the extent that I wasn't even paying enough attention to my own daughter.

"Well, I think it's a tell-tale sign that there must be a

new guy in her life. Wouldn't that be exciting?"

"Shhh --- here she comes!" I whispered as Macy took her seat at the table with a definite smile on her face and a gleam in her eye as she glanced across the table at me.

"Okay, Macy. Spill it," Kelly blurted out. "Was that a guy?"

Macy's cheeks turned four shades of pink. "Yeah, his name is Tony. He's just a friend from culinary school. He may come visit and help me with the bakery planning."

"Well, how nice of him! I look forward to meeting any of your friends from school." I smiled at Macy. I could tell there was probably more to it than that, but I let it go for now. I was sure she would share more when she was ready.

I directed the conversation back to the investigation and see if I could get any more info from Jake. "How well do you know Megan Lester and her husband?" I asked, remembering the comments about the condo development.

"Pretty well. Her husband, Chris, owns the Sweetwater Herald and is on the city council. They have a huge house on the lake. I think it's on Edgewater Road. Why?"

"I walked into a conversation at the Ladies' Club meeting about the rumor of Terrance Wolfe's condo development. I got the feeling that it could become a real messy issue if he finds a way to move forward."

"Oh, it will definitely be a mess. Business owners will benefit, but lake landowners won't like it at all."

"Megan even commented that Terrance had better watch his back, because it could get violent. Of course, now that J.R. is dead, Terrance may drop the whole idea."

"What are you saying, Glory? You can't possibly think Chris Lester would kill J.R. just to stop a condo development. That's just crazy!"

"Well, I thought so too until I talked with Jolene at the Lake House Café today at lunch. She said that Chris met someone late Saturday night for drinks and she overheard bits and pieces of the conversation."

Jake adjusted himself in his chair and sat forward. "Go on."

"She overheard Chris trying to talk Sam Baylor into selling him some property, I'm assuming so he could keep Terrance and J.R. from building condos on it."

"I know Sam was an old friend of J.R. and Linda, but what does he have to do with any property? Does he even own property here?"

"It's a long story, but he feels like he will soon inherit some property that Terrance is interested in."

"Did she hear Sam's response?"

"Just that he didn't own the property yet, but that when he did it would go to the highest bidder."

"Hmmm . . . I think I might need to have a talk with Chris Lester. I still can't believe that he would kill over something like that, though." Jake frowned.

"It was just a thought. Megan was pretty adamant about it and you have to admit that it could cause people to lose a lot of money. People have killed for less." I decided not to volunteer the information about Terrance and Jeannie or Sam Baylor's family past just yet. I still wanted to see if I could collect a few more pieces to the puzzle. Somehow they all had to be connected to J.R.'s death. I just needed to figure out who had the strongest reason for wanting J.R. dead. I didn't want to send Jake down a rabbit hole and waste his time on something that had no connection to the investigation. I needed to confirm a few more things before I filled him in.

"Macy, this lemon cake is delicious!" Jake said, scraping the last few crumbs off his plate with his fork. "Will this be on the menu in the bakery?"

I jerked my head up and glared playfully at him. "I'll have you know, I made that cake!"

"No way. I've tasted your attempts at baking before," he laughed.

"Well, I admit, Macy walked me through the recipe, but I did most of it." I crossed my arms across my chest and pouted.

"She really did!" Macy interjected. "All I did was instruct!"

I smiled, glowing with pride.

"Well, I'm impressed! Oh, and speaking of impressed, Chief Detective Walker had quite a few things to say about you after your little visit the other day. I think you made quite an impression on him." Jake loaded up his plate with a second slice of cake.

"Not sure if that's a good thing or a bad thing. He struck me as definitely all business. I'm not sure he even looked up from the file he was writing in the whole time I was answering his questions."

"Oh, he definitely looked up." Jake said with a sly grin.

"What do you mean? I was only in there five minutes. Surely, I couldn't have offended him in that amount of time." I reached for my glass of tea and took a drink.

"Oh, you didn't offend him. I think intrigued might be

a better word. He was asking me all sorts of questions about you." I saw Jake make eye contact with Macy and her eyebrows rose.

"What did you tell him about me?"

"I just told him to stay as far away from you as he could, and he should be fine." Jake winked. "Just kidding, I told him you were a strong-willed, hard-working, fun-loving Alabama girl that was glad to be back home."

I felt an unexplained heat rising to my cheeks, "Well, I hope I have no reason to be back in his office, but thanks for the vote of confidence, little brother."

"What kind of questions was he asking?" I shifted in my chair.

"Mostly personal things, like if you were married and what your interests are. He asked where you lived before moving back to Alabama."

"Why would he care about things like that?" I heard my voice crack as the heat rose in my cheeks.

"He seemed really interested in the fact that you lived in Texas. He's originally from Texas, so I guess he just felt like you might have something in common."

"Sounds like I may have to keep an eye on both Harper ladies," Kelly waggled her eyebrows at Macy and then at me.

I rolled my eyes. "I've got way too many irons in the fire right now to even think about anything like that. I'm sure he was just making polite conversation."

I felt every eye at the table glued on me, so I promptly got up and started clearing dishes, hopefully indicating that this subject of discussion was officially closed.

CHAPTER 12

Since everyone was so exhausted from the crazy week, we decided to make it an early night. Kelly and Jake thanked us for supper and headed home. I was still so wound up, there was no way I could sleep, so I decided to walk out on the porch and call Momma to see if she heard anything interesting at Rummy Club.

"Did you get any new information about any of our suspects?" I ask Momma as I rocked and enjoyed the night air.

"I fished around with a few questions. Lucy Craig almost choked on her tea when I said how bad I felt for Terrance losing his business partner and good friend. She said she heard that Terrance has been making some less than flattering comments about J.R. and how J.R. thought he was the one who runs the business. Jolene evidently told Lucy the same thing she told us, that Terrance got pretty tipsy last week at Goldiggers and said some cruel things about J.R. Things like he wished he could get that business to himself and he'd really show everyone how a business should be run. He claimed he'd have it making double the money in no time."

"So nothing new there. Anything else?"

"I talked some more with Bonnie. She does Jeannie's hair, I didn't make a comment about the bad dye job, and according to her, business has really been good lately, but she said Terrance has big plans and lots of ideas for the business to make it even better. She got the impression he'd do just about anything to push J.R. to expand the business."

"Sounds like this just confirms the impression we got from Jeannie today as well as what we learned from Jolene."

"Martha Jean said she had heard that J.R. had a temper. He threatened Jeffery Walker, who sacks groceries at the Piggly Wiggly when he accused Jeffery of looking at Linda a little too long when he was putting the grocery bags in the car. He said J.R. grabbed him by the shirt and slammed him up against the car. She said in her opinion, J.R. might have been just a little too high strung."

"Do you think it's possible that the killer was someone that he crossed? Maybe we're too set on making this about Linda or about the property. What if it's totally unrelated? Maybe he just made the wrong person mad."

"I guess it's possible, but I still think our top suspects are the ones we already have on the list. That's about all I was able to get out of the ladies tonight. Bonnie did say she felt sorry Linda."

"What did she mean by that?" I asked.

"Well, the last time she trimmed up her hair, Linda looked troubled and Bonnie said she could see bruises on her face that she had tried to cover up with makeup. She asked her what happened, and she just said that she tripped and fell working in her yard."

"That also goes along with the comments that her mother made to us yesterday. Thanks for filling me in, Momma. I sure hate to hear that J.R. wasn't the person I always thought he was. It really makes me sad."

* * *

Wednesday morning started with a bang when I went out to get in my car to head to work and saw that my back tire was flat. I got the spare out and Macy helped me change it. I didn't want to scare Macy, but on closer inspection, it looked like it had been slashed.

"Mom, this doesn't look like just a flat tire. It looks like it might have been done by someone intentionally. Promise me you will watch yourself and who's around you. Don't get caught in a bad situation. Dad got you a handgun for protection, didn't he?" Macy said, sounding more like the parent than the child.

"Yes, I have one in the nightstand drawer. After you went off to college, your dad made me take the class with him, so I would feel better about staying alone when he had to travel for work."

"Good. Then you need to put your gun in your purse. You got that carry permit for a reason. So you can carry it, not leave it at home in the nightstand."

"Ok, but please don't worry about me. Maybe I just ran over something or scraped the curb. I'm sure it's nothing to worry about or just a bunch of kids out looking for trouble to get into," I said with more conviction than I really felt.

Macy filled my travel mug with coffee as I was getting my things together for work. "I'm going to be working at the bakery most of the day but I'll get cleaned up and be at church in time for supper. One of the girls I met at the Ladies' Club and I are going out for coffee after Bible study."

"Sounds like a plan. I'll see you then."

"Mom, be careful." She hugged me and I left for the office.

The tire fiasco had me running late for work. I called Momma on my way to the office." Are you coming to J.R.'s funeral service this afternoon? I think it's at two here at the church." I asked.

"Yes, I plan on it. I want to support Linda and Matthew. You know our Sunday school class is bringing potluck lunch for the family after the service, so I'm about to put on a pot of green beans and bake an apple pie. I'll see you then."

The church was on the other side of town which took all of five minutes to get to. Main Street in Sweetwater Springs was unusually busy this Wednesday morning. Many storefronts were being renovated and given a facelift all up and down the street. It gave me a warm feeling on the inside to know how much the people here love their town and wanted it to grow and prosper. Excitement rose and I couldn't keep from smiling as I drove past the old furniture store, which would soon become Macy's on Main Hometown Bakery and Beanery.

As I continued down Main Street and turned left onto

Sycamore Avenue, I was mentally checking off my to do list for the day. The church was built in a beautiful traditional style with stately white columns out front and a towering steeple that stood tall over the grove of poplar and sycamore trees that surrounded it and the graveyard next door. The steeple housed a beautiful old bell that Pastor Dan still made sure to ring each Sunday morning just before the start of the service. Everything was in bloom. Spring has definitely sprung. The pollen had painted every car in the parking lot a dull shade of yellow. I checked the supply of tissues and allergy meds in my purse and headed across the parking lot, remotely locking the car behind me with a loud beep.

I always parked around back in the parking lot next to the graveyard. The parking lot was quiet. All the crime scene tape had been removed and you'd be hard pressed to see anything out of the ordinary. I entered through the back door as usual.

"Mornin' Glory!" chimed Pastor Dan as I walked through the door. "I hope you have recovered from the shock of recent events."

"Good morning to you too." I said as I put my purse away and booted up my computer screen.

"Yes, it's certainly going to take me awhile to come in here and not get a creepy feeling, but I'm sure it will eventually get back to normal."

The church office was pretty large considering the small size of the church itself. There was a large open room with a pretty little sitting area over to the left with a gray sofa, a leather armchair and a side table. The door to the left led to Pastor Dan's office and a door to the right led to the workroom with copier, folding machine and plenty of workspace and storage. Just off that room there was a small room with a table and chairs that was used for file storage and counting the offering. That's where the safe drawer was located. It was really about the size of a large walk-in closet, but it served its purpose well. I said a silent thankful prayer that the money in the safe hadn't been taken and that the offering donations in the bank bag would somehow be recovered.

My desk sat right up front and faced the office door. Pastor Dan had hired me six months ago when the last secretary, Maynelle Barnes, retired after working there for thirty years. Mrs. Maynelle was not the computering sort, so I had been slowly trying to drag the office into the twenty-first century. Short, slender and gray-haired, Pastor Dan was getting on in years, but he was pretty tech savvy for his age. He could use a computer and would occasionally tweet out his favorite Bible verse of the day. I still typed up his sermons, but he answered his own emails. The only other employees of the church were Jason Taylor and Carl Weeks. Jason was the Choir Director as well as a Youth Leader. Being a small church in a small town often leads to small budgets, so he was doing double duty for the time being. Carl was the custodian and general go-to guy for whatever anyone needed.

I had to hit the ground running when I finally made it to my desk. What was left of the morning flew by in a flurry of trying to get a week's worth of work done in one day. Luckily, with the big celebration last Sunday, we didn't have Sunday school classes, so I didn't have to post that attendance. That was one less thing on my list. The only big thing I had left to do was the bulletin handout for this Sunday, so I got to work on that.

When I finally took a breather and glanced up at the office clock, I realized it was already noon. I decided to take a quick break and stretch my legs. I grabbed my lunch and took it outside to the picnic tables under the shade trees. I knew today would be a busy day because I had so much catching up to do, so I had packed an insulated lunch bag with a turkey and provolone sandwich on a croissant, a small bag of grapes and a bottle of water.

I walked outside and saw Carl taking a lunch break also. This was my chance to ask him a few questions about the Sunday services. He is not only the church custodian, but he's a member of the Sunday security team. The team consists of a couple of guys who patrol the church buildings and grounds during the services.

"Hi, Carl, mind if I join you? It's so pretty out here today." I took a seat and unzipped my lunch bag.

"Not at all! I could use the company. I'm still kinda overwhelmed from the whole murder thing."

"I've been meaning to ask you a question, since I know you are on the security team. Did you happen to see anything out of the ordinary Sunday? I mean, aside from the fact that it wasn't a normal Sunday to begin with."

"I've been going over and over it in my mind and I think I did remember something, but I don't know if it has anything to do with the killer."

"You never know. What is it?"

"Well, I noticed a car parked in the no parking zone near the back entrance. It was probably just someone who was running late for church and didn't want to have to park on the back side of Egypt and walk all the way through the graveyard. I thought it was odd that I didn't remember it being there earlier in the service. We try to keep a watch on that since it's a law to keep that area clear in case we have an emergency. I went to your office and got a yellow sticky note and pen off your desk and wrote them a note asking them to please not park there in the future. I went out and put it on their windshield."

"What did the car look like?"

"It was a dark blue sedan of some kind. I was going to write down the tag number, but I realized that I had left the pen lying on your desk."

"Do you remember seeing anyone around it or near my office?" I took a bite of my sandwich.

"No, there wasn't anyone near your office when I was there unless they were in the restroom."

"What time was that?"

"I'd say about midway through the service. The choir had just finished, and Pastor Dan was just starting his sermon. I remember because that's my normal routine. That's when I make my pass through that side of the building every Sunday."

"So halfway through the service, the car was there and by the time church service was over, it was gone?"

"Yes. It was definitely gone after the service because that's where the ambulance parked when we called 911."

"Carl, I think you might have seen the killer's car!" I said feeling like this could be an important new clue.

"Did you tell Jake any of this?"

"No, actually, it didn't even occur to me that it could've been connected until I was sitting out here rehashing the whole awful scenario. I guess I was too shook up at the time to think about it."

"I'm going to call Jake and let him know. He may want to ask you some more questions about it. Let me know if you remember anything else."

"I will. I guess I need to get back to work. Enjoy the rest of your lunch."

I popped a grape in my mouth as I scrolled down to find Jake's number in my cell phone.

I frowned when the call went straight to voicemail, so I left him a message to call me back. I was frustrated that I couldn't follow up on the new lead immediately. It would have to wait until later. I decided to try to relax for a few more minutes before I had to get back to work.

Sitting under the trees, it was hard not to let my mind wander to the last time I was out here. Such a lovely place marred by such a horrific event. When I walked in the office this morning, I knew that it would take me awhile not to picture what must have happened in there. The shock on J.R.'s face when he faced his killer. I shook my head to try to clear it and focus on the beautiful weather. Gazing up into the clouds and the beautiful blue sky, I prayed for resolution and quick justice. I was more determined than ever to find out more about J.R.'s relationships with the people around him.

CHAPTER 13

"*A*re you coming to the service?" I looked up from my desk to see Pastor Dan heading toward the office door.

"Is it two o'clock already? Yes, I'm right behind you. I'll lock the office door while we're all in the other part of the building."

The service was short. The music Linda had chosen was nice and Pastor Dan gave a very comforting sermon. It seemed that Linda was doing as well as could be expected. Her mother was sitting next to her holding Matthew in her lap and I noticed the man I had seen in church Sunday sitting on her other side. Since I still had not met him in person, I could only assume that was Sam Baylor. Terrence and Jeannie were sitting a few rows in front of me.

As soon as the crowd was dismissed to the graveside service, I hurried to catch up with Terrance and Jeannie. "Hi, Jeannie. I don't know if you remember me. My mom and I came by Monday morning."

"Sure, I remember. Glory, right?" Popping her gum, she shot me an uninterested glance.

I turned to Terrance. "I'm sorry, I haven't met you yet. My name is Glory Harper. I'm the church secretary here. I came by Monday to express my condolences about J.R.'s death."

He nodded. "Thank you. Yes, it's been pretty crazy this week trying to contact all his clients and make sure all his sales paperwork has been filed."

"I'm sure it has. Jeannie mentioned that you'd been stressed lately with one of your listings and now you have all this to deal with, too."

He cut his eyes over at Jeannie and she looked down suddenly very interested in her nails.

"She also said you are looking at a new condo venture out on the lake. That sounds really nice."

"Jeannie seems to be a wealth of information." He frowned. Jeannie turned to walk away and he grabbed her hand and tugged her back to his side, making sure she stayed put.

"I understand that J.R. was against expanding the business to include rental properties and didn't support your condo project idea. Is that what the fight outside your office was about? That must have made you pretty mad at him."

"Listen, lady, if you're implying that I had anything to do with his death, you're way off base. Sure, I was mad, but I'd never do anything like that."

"Well, that's good to hear. One last question."

He blew out a long breath and stared at me. "What is it?"

"On Friday, a man called the church office looking for J.R. and I directed him to the realty office. Jeannie said that he did in fact come by. His name was Sam Baylor."

"Yes, he came in and surprised J.R. with a visit. I think he was an old college friend. We talked for a bit until J.R. returned from showing a house. I saw him sitting next to Linda in the service. Crazy coincidence -- I found out that I have his aunt's home and property listed right now."

"Does that happen to be the property you are hoping to use for the condos?"

"Yes, it is. But she refuses to come off the price and I couldn't swing it without J.R. being on board. So you see, that's one more reason for me to NOT want J.R. dead. I needed him to make this work. The last time I talked to him, he actually seemed like he was warming up to the idea. He said he needed to check into some financial things, and he would consider it and let me know next week."

"OK. Thank you for taking a minute to talk with me."

I stopped by the fellowship hall on the way back to my office after I left Terrance and Jeannie. Momma was in there setting out the food for the family.

"Did you see Sam sitting next to Linda? Looks like he's moving in pretty quickly."

She nodded as she placed serving spoons next to each dish. "I'm not sure if that makes him more suspicious in my eyes or less. Maybe he's just being kind because he loves her."

I nodded. "I guess you're right. It could be that." I have always tried to be the kind of person that gave people the benefit of the doubt. I never wanted to be a person who judged someone without knowing all the facts. I realized that, since the murder, I was quickly becoming someone I didn't like. "I have to get back in the office and finish up the bulletin, but I'll see you at supper tonight here at church."

"I'll save you and Macy a seat."

* * *

The time on my computer monitor read 5 o'clock and I was more than ready to go for the day. I straightened my desk and put files away. It was Italian night for family night supper at the church and the enticing smells of spaghetti and garlic bread were calling my name. I loved being able to walk down the hall to a nice supper and have a night off from cooking. I went through the serving line and grabbed a seat at the table with Momma, Macy and Kelly.

A couple of older ladies joined us at the table. Momma introduced them to me as Lynette Weeks and Margie Baker. Of course, they remembered me, but I didn't really remember them. They went on and on about how they couldn't believe how Annie's little girl had grown up and had a daughter of her own. After a little conversation, I learned that Lynette has worked in the loan department at the bank for many years. As casually as I could, I guided the conversation to the growth of our city and new businesses and the loans those new businesses invariably need.

"I have been hearing some rumors about a condo development on the lake. Have y'all heard anything about that?"

Margie nodded and took a drink of her iced tea. "My son works for Graham Construction and he said they had already been contacted by J.R. to submit a bid so that he could get an idea of the kind of money he was gonna have to potentially come up with."

"I did hear something about that," Lynette added, "But I have no idea if it will happen now. J.R. Jenkins met with the loan officer about something related to that, but now that he's gone, I guess he won't need that loan after all. So sad." Lynette and Margie both shook their heads.

How convenient. I thought to myself.

I was still humming the tune to the hymn we sang in Bible study when I turned onto our street. I glanced in the rearview mirror and realized that the same car had been behind me since I left the church parking lot and had turned onto the street also. I decided to keep driving and see if they followed. I drove right past our driveway and turned the corner to make the block, trying not to look too obvious looking in my rearview mirror. They dropped back but were definitely still there. I turned into the driveway and mentally smacked myself on the forehead for forgetting to leave the porch light on again. The house was pitch black and so was most of the street. The only streetlight was about three houses down, so it didn't give us much light. I remembered that Macy was meeting her friend for coffee, so I knew I was on my own. I sat in the car for a few seconds saying a quick prayer for protection, then got my keys in my hand and quickly got out of the car, practically running up the porch steps. I fumbled the key into the lock, stepped in and shut the door behind me. After locking the deadbolt and turning on the lights, I pulled back the living room curtain just the least little bit and looked between the crack in the blinds. The car was still there, parked in front of the house next door. I could see the shape of someone sitting in the driver's seat. I couldn't tell if it was a man or woman, but it looked like whoever it was, had on a dark hoodie pulled up over their head and had sunglasses on. If I hadn't been so terrified, I probably would have thought it crazy attire for Alabama in May --- at night. But that didn't really occur to me because my brain was frozen. I found my cell phone in my purse and speed-dialed Jake.

"Hey Sis, what's up?"

"Someone followed me home from church. They are still sitting in front of the house watching me," I said barely able to breathe.

"What? Why would anyone do that? Are you sure they aren't just visiting someone in the neighborhood?"

"No, Jake. It looks like they are watching the house. I don't recognize the car, but it looks like they have on a dark hoodie and sunglasses."

"What kind of car? Can you see the tag number?"

"It's a dark blue sedan of some kind. Maybe a Toyota Corolla or something? You know I don't know car models. They all look alike to me. And it's parked facing me, so I can't see the tag."

"OK, I'm on my way. Stay in the house, make sure all the doors are locked and stay away from the windows.

"OK. Thanks."

I disconnected the call and gathered Izzy up in my arms and sat down to wait. It seemed like an hour, but I'm sure it was more like five minutes when someone started banging on my door. I jumped out of my skin and Izzy scrambled out of my lap and went crazy barking.

"Glory! Are you OK?" Jake hollered.

I unlocked the door and let him in. "Yes, I'm fine. Did you see them?"

"No, the car was gone by the time I got here. Where's Macy?"

"She met a friend for coffee after church."

"Can you please tell me why on earth do you think someone might have a reason to follow you? You haven't been nosing around in my investigation anymore, have you?"

"Well, I might have asked a few questions around town. Maybe someone got spooked? Maybe I'm getting too close for comfort? I might as well tell you because I'm sure Macy will if I don't, but I think someone slashed my tire last night. It was flat this morning when I got ready to leave."

"You have to stop it right now. I mean it, Glory. If this person that followed you tonight is the same person who killed J.R., then you could be in real danger."

"I know. I'm sorry. I promise I'll be more careful."

"I know how hard-headed you are, so I know I can't force you to do anything, but I'm asking you as your brother to please be careful who you talk to and what situations you put yourself in. Do you understand? I love you."

"I promise. I love you too."

"I'll put out a BOLO for a dark blue sedan around town, but that's a pretty vague description. Is there anything else you can remember about the car?"

"It was waiting to pull out of the Quik Stop across from the church parking lot when I was leaving choir practice. I didn't really think anything about it at the time, but I think that's when they pulled out behind me."

I closed my eyes to try to envision the car sitting there at the station and tried to remember anything distinctive about it. "I really can't think of anything unusual about it. It was just a blue car."

"Maybe I can go by the Quik Stop and see if they have security cameras. Maybe they got a shot of the driver or the tag." He said hopefully.

"Wait!! I almost forgot! When I called you today at lunch and left you that voice mail, I had been visiting with Carl during our lunch break and he remembered something about Sunday that he hadn't told you."

"I'm sorry I didn't call you back. It's been crazy at the station. What did he tell you?"

"He's on the security team and he makes his rounds to the back side of the building and office area about halfway through the service. He said just as Pastor Dan was starting the sermon, he walked out the back entrance and noticed a car parked in the no parking area. He figured it was just someone running late for church who didn't want to park so far away. He went to my office and borrowed a sticky note and pen and left a note on their windshield. He forgot the pen in my office so he couldn't write down the tag number. He didn't think about it again, but now realizes that it was gone when the service was over because the no parking area was empty when the ambulance pulled up. He said it was a blue sedan!" I was talking ninety to nothing and stopped to take a long breath. "Do you think it could be the car that followed me home tonight?"

"It sounds very possible. I know you've been asking a lot of questions around town. Tell me who all you've talked to. You must have made someone very antsy."

"Well, of course Linda and her momma. You already knew about that. I also talked to Brigette at the flower shop about Linda & J.R.'s relationship. I'm sure it's not her." I said, trying to mentally scan down the list of suspects I had questioned.

"Who else?"

"Momma and I stopped in at the realty office. Terrance wasn't there but we chatted with Jeannie for a few minutes. I did talk to Terrance today after the funeral, though."

"How did he seem to you?"

"He seemed a little perturbed with Jeannie for sharing too much information with me, but other than that, he seemed genuinely upset over J.R.'s death."

"What kind of information did she share with you that he didn't like?"

"Just that he was having trouble with a pushy client and was hoping to buy some property to start the condo project. But, she said that Terrance had big plans for the business that J.R wanted no part of."

"Anything else you can think of?"

"Well, I don't think he knows that she let it slip to me and Momma, but she and Terrance are dating and she was with him on the boat Sunday."

"What? Why wouldn't he tell me that when I asked him for an alibi?"

"She said he thought it was best if no one knew about their relationship just yet. He didn't think it looked professional to be dating his receptionist. She said she met him for lunch on the boat and was with him the rest of the day."

"Ok, well, that may or may not give him an alibi. Depending on what time she got to the boat, it's possible that he still could've killed J.R. and made it there before she arrived," Jake said.

"Momma and I tried to visit Sam Baylor out at the Lakeside Motel, but he wasn't in his room." I left out the part about breaking and entering. I didn't think that would go over very well. "I also talked to the ladies at the Ladies' Club meeting. I already told you about Megan Lester's comments. Let's see . . ." I said tapping my finger to my chin, "Oh, yeah, and Jolene down at the Lake Shore Café told us about Chris Lester meeting with Sam. I think that's about it."

"Well I have to say, you and Momma sure do get around. You've had the opportunity to make a lot of people uneasy with all your curiosity. We've talked with most of these people already and I don't think any of them drive a blue sedan. But maybe it will lead to something we haven't considered."

"Can you walk out in the backyard with me to let Izzy

do her business before you go? I know she's ready to go out!" I asked sheepishly.

"Sure," Jake smiled.

I hugged his neck and thanked him again for coming to my rescue.

CHAPTER 14

A few minutes after Jake left, I saw headlights flash through the front window and across the room and I prayed that it was Macy turning into the driveway. I could hear her on her cell phone as she got out of the car and walked up the front steps to the door and I could tell from the conversation that she was talking to her Uncle Jake.

"Mom, why didn't you call me?" She fussed before she even got through the front door. "I would've come straight home and met you here! Surely, they wouldn't have tried anything with both of us. I couldn't bear it if something happened to you!"

"I probably should have called you while I was driving around the block, but I was just so focused on the car and trying to get into the house and lock the door, I just didn't think about it. I'm sorry if I worried you!" I said apologetically. I hugged her close. "And your Uncle Jake is a blabbermouth!" I said with a grin. "I'm sure whoever it was, was just trying to scare me. If they had wanted to hurt me,

they would have done it before Jake got here. I must be
getting too close for comfort to whoever is responsible
for all of this."

The next morning, Macy slept in. She was just about
worn out from all the work on the bakery this week. She
wasn't used to this much manual labor. I sat on the back
patio with my Bible and coffee.

*"God blesses those who work for peace, for they will be called the
children of God."* Matthew 5:9

I prayed that I would be a person who would work for
peace. That God would help me know which way to focus
my investigation to help Jake the most so that we could
have peace in our town again.

As I closed my Bible and headed into the house, my
cell buzzed a text from Momma.

*"I think we need to talk to Sam. He's the one suspect we
haven't spoken to face to face."*

I texted her back. *"I agree. Be there in half an hour."*

* * *

"Let's head to the motel." I said as I turned down the
highway towards the lake. "We can try our church visit
again."

On the way to the motel, I told Momma about being
followed home from church last night and the flat tire
yesterday morning and I reassured her that Jake was
checking it out and watching out for me.

"Glory, I will be the first to admit that I was excited

about this adventure. I think I took it a little too casually. I never truly thought it would get dangerous. From here on out, we need to be really careful."

I nodded in agreement as we rounded the curve and approached the motel. Turning into the motel parking lot, I drove straight to the back of the building toward Room 11. There was a truck parked in the #11 parking space, so hopefully that meant Sam was in his room.

Momma knocked softly on the door. The door cracked open and a voice came from inside the room. "Yes?"

"Hello! We're from Sweetwater Springs Baptist Church just dropping by to thank you for visiting our church Sunday morning!" Momma said with her best church lady smile. "May we come in?"

"We won't take up much of your time." I smiled sweetly and stuck my foot in the doorway forcing Sam to step back and let us in.

"I'm Glory Harper and this is my momma, Annie Miller."

"Sam Baylor." He said shaking my hand.

"I knew your name sounded familiar. I'm the church secretary. I think I spoke to you one day last week. Didn't you call the church office asking about J.R. and Linda Jenkins?"

"Uh. . . yes, I think I did."

"It's so terrible what happened to J.R. Did you get to see them before the . . . uh . . . I mean, before it all happened?"

"Yes, I saw them the day I talked to you. I stopped by his office and J.R. invited me home for dinner with him and Linda that evening. I was shocked to find out they had a little boy. I didn't realize that. I haven't seen them since their wedding about three and a half years ago."

"Were y'all close? I'm sorry if I'm being nosy, but I'm just hoping that Linda has someone she can lean on during this time for her and Matthew." I asked, hoping to get an idea of his feelings for Linda. At least I knew now that he had no idea that he had a son until he arrived in town.

"Yes, we used to be really close. J.R. had changed a lot though. Linda said he was moody and really angry a lot of the time. Work was really stressing him out." Sam continued. "I have some other business in the area to tend to, so I'll be around for awhile longer. I plan to check on Linda from time to time."

"Didn't I see you sitting next to her at the funeral yesterday?"

Sam nervously shifted his weight from side to side. "Yes, she asked me to sit there. I didn't want people to get the wrong idea, but she said she didn't care. She was ready to move forward."

"Do you see yourself moving here to our little piece of Alabama heaven?" I hoped I could just get him to admit to looking for the property. I wasn't sure how that all fit together, but I felt like it was a very important piece of the puzzle.

"My family owns some land in the area, so I thought I might check it out while I'm here. My aunt owns it right now, but she's getting older and when she passes it will be mine. I was just curious to see it since it could be mine soon."

"I see. I'm sure that will be nice to have your own place." I commented, wondering if he might be getting just a little ahead of himself. How was he so sure it would be his sooner rather than later? "Just out of curiosity, has anyone approached you about buying the property from you?"

"As a matter of fact, a guy named Chris Lester asked to meet with me about it last weekend. I just told him that it wasn't mine to sell and when it was, I'd be glad to consider any offers. I'm not really interested in the house, just the property and what goes with it."

"Well, thank you for your time. We just wanted to say welcome to our neck of the woods." We both waved as he closed the door behind us.

It was getting close to noon and my stomach rumbled, reminding me that neither of us had eaten any breakfast. Just coffee. "Let's go back to my house and have some lunch. I need to let Izzy out anyway." I suggested.

"Sounds good to me! My puppies are growling, too!" Momma said. I couldn't help but laugh. That was what my Granny always said when she was hungry. Momma was so much like her and I loved it.

When we arrived at the house, Macy's vehicle was nowhere to be seen. I supposed she had errands to run. Izzy met us at the door jumping and wiggling her tail. Momma bent over and scratched her behind the ears and made baby talk.

"I'll start getting lunch. Will you let her out into the back yard for a minute?"

Momma opened the door and Izzy zoomed out, stopping to sniff out every bug and cricket she could find. I read once that to a dog, sniffing around is like reading the newspaper for humans. They get to find out who's been by to say hello and what's going on in the neighborhood, so I try not to rush her if she's having a good time doing her own type of investigation.

As I got out bowls and spoons and warmed up the left-over Hodge Podge soup from supper the night before, I noticed a note on the countertop saying Macy had to run up to the bakery. The plumbers were there, and they had some questions for her and she would be back soon.

"Sorry there isn't any Mexican cornbread left! Jake ate the last of it. But I have plenty of crackers." I heard a scratch at the back door that signaled Izzy had finished her business and wanted to visit with company. "I've been thinking . . . Sam sounded pretty sure he was going to own that property soon. That makes me think that he's getting impatient for that necklace. That's a very expensive emerald and diamond necklace. Whoever gets the house, gets that necklace which is easily worth more than the house."

Momma's face looked worried, "Do you think that Judith could be in danger? Would he really harm his own aunt over a necklace?"

"If he thought she was going to sell off that property before he inherited it, that might make him want to speed up the process."

"Let's go over our suspect list one more time." I got out my notepad as I blew across a spoonful of my steaming soup to cool it off.

"I think there's a chance that we might need to add a suspect to the list that we haven't considered before. I don't really have a name, but I think it may be possible that J.R. was killed to either stop the condo deal from getting off the ground or to send a message to Terrance to just drop the whole idea."

"I can see that," Momma absentmindedly stirred her soup while she thought. "Who do you think it could have been?"

"I certainly don't want to point fingers just yet, but Megan Lester sure seemed to insinuate that possibility at the meeting. Do you think Chris Lester or any other landowners that would stoop that low? For now, let's just keep an open mind about it."

Momma nodded, "I think we can mark Linda off the list as a suspect. He left her no insurance money and she's really worse off than she was before."

"I agree. Also, Jake told me last night that her mother has an alibi. She was at her own church service that morning at the Methodist church. That should be easy enough to verify, so we can mark her off too."

"What about Jeannie?" I tapped my pencil on the notepad. "Is she covering for Terrance? If she didn't get to the boat dock until twelve thirty, is it still possible that Terrance killed J.R and went straight to his boat to meet her? She might not even realize she could be giving Terrance a false alibi."

"That leaves us with Terrance and Sam," Momma stated.

"Let's also think about what kind of cars they drive. Maybe that can help us narrow it down."

"Someone at the realty office drives a yellow Mustang.

One of those that looks like a bumble bee. I saw it parked in front of the office."

"Terrance drives a little red sports car of some kind, so that must be Jeannie's Mustang and Sam drives a truck. I'm not sure what Chris Lester drives."

"OK, here's what we know," I started to read off the notes from my notepad. "Terrance wants the business for himself and wants to expand. He also wants that Lindsey property. But the fact that J.R. had begun to change his tune about the deal shines a new light on his motive, don't you think? He said he needed J.R. to be in on the deal for it to have any hope of going through. If that's true and J.R. had changed his mind and was no longer fighting Terrance on the idea, he may not have as strong a motive as we thought."

"If he's been snooping around out there alone, it's very possible he could have found the necklace. That would be motive enough to try to get the property for himself." Momma said.

"Either way, he wants that property and getting rid of J.R. gives him the opportunity to do what he wants with the business and he wouldn't have to share that necklace." I agreed.

"Sam wants Linda and Matthew," I said, moving on to the last name on the list. "He also wants to get that property and the necklace before Judith has a chance to sell it. I figure he wants to use the money from the necklace to start a new life for the three of them."

"If Sam is the killer, do you think he might confront Judith at the motel? Do you think we need to go out there to warn her that she might be in danger?" Momma looked concerned. "There's no telling what he might do if he sees Judith when she arrives and realizes he may be running out of time."

I looked down at the notepad. Absentmindedly doodling on the paper, I had written *SAM* in capital letters on the paper. *Judith in danger? Motel 2pm* and circled it all. "Jeannie said Judith's flight was supposed to arrive just before two, and Terrance is picking her up at two thirty. If we time it just right, maybe we can get to her as soon as she gets there and before Sam sees her."

I looked up and jumped as Macy walked in. "Hey, you two! What are y'all up to today? Or do I even want to know?" She cocked an eyebrow and smiled.

"Not much. We thought we might take a drive out to Lakeside Motel this afternoon."

"Who's out there you're wanting to see? Momma, if y'all are still playing detective you better be really careful. I would say I'd go with you, but unfortunately, I have to go back to the bakery to meet with the plumber again in an hour, so I can't tag along," Macy said.

"We're not getting into any trouble," I said, hoping I wasn't lying. "Judith Lindsey is staying there and we're hoping she might have some information that would help with the case. We were just going to have a little visit. The lady's like eighty years old. I promise we'll be safe."

I put our dishes in the sink and kissed her on the head. "Will you let Izzy out one more time before you head to the bakery?"

"I will. Please promise me you will be careful?" Macy looked me in the eye.

"I promise." We waved and walked out the door.

CHAPTER 15

"*D*o you think we should stop by Sweetwater Springs Realty and tell Terrance about Sam? If Judith is in danger, he may need to know what they're walking into." Momma asked.

Realizing she was right, I swung the Honda into an empty spot in front of Bonnie's Cut and Curl. The bell on the realty office door jingled as we walked in. The front office was empty. No cheerful welcome from Jeannie. I looked around and walked toward the hall and back office that I snooped through a few days ago.

"Hello? Hello?"

Terrance's office door opened. "Oh, it's you again. I'm sorry, I didn't hear you with my door closed. What can I do for you today? Here with more questions I suppose?" His voice dripped with sarcasm.

"We were hoping to talk with you and Jeannie for just a moment. Is she here today?"

"No, her Mustang has been in the shop for a couple of

days and she needed to pick it up and return the rental she's been driving, so it's just me this afternoon. I have to meet a client in just a bit, but I still have a few minutes."

"That's what we wanted to talk with you about."

Terrance furrowed his brow. "I'm sorry, I'm not following you. Are you interested in looking at that property?"

"No, nothing like that. Jeannie mentioned that the owner was coming to town today and the two of you were going to look at the property together."

"Yes, that's correct, but why would that be any business of yours if you aren't interested in the house?"

"We have been talking with a few people around town about the events leading up to J.R.'s death. We think there may be a connection between the fact that Sam Baylor is an heir to the Lindsey property and J.R.'s death. Judith Lindsey may be in danger. If she is trying to sell the property and Sam is the rightful heir, he may do whatever it takes to keep her from selling."

"What are you saying? You think he might harm his own aunt?"

"That's exactly what I'm saying. Sam is staying at the motel also. I think we may need to get to the motel before he has an opportunity to intercept Judith and possibly threaten or harm her."

"I'm supposed to meet her at two thirty. That gives us forty five minutes. Let's go ahead to the motel and make sure that she is safe. That lady is crazy as a bat, but I would feel terrible if anything happened to her. Y'all follow me to the motel and we'll check on her."

"Hopefully we'll be just in time to catch Judith as she arrives at the motel." I said to Momma as we pulled up to the motel office. "Hi Josie, could you tell me if you have a lady staying here named Judith Lindsey?"

"Sure, do. She arrived about fifteen minutes ago but you just missed her." Josie must have realized from the look on my face that something was wrong. "Oh dear, what's the matter? She had a message waiting when she arrived that Terrance was tied up with a client and she should take a taxi to the house and he would meet her there."

"I never sent her that message!" Terrance's face paled.

"We need to find her and make sure she's safe. Thank you! We'll explain later, Josie!"

Edgewater Road was a narrow, very curvy two-lane. My Honda held the turns as I zoomed as fast as I dared, trying my best to keep up with Terrance in his red sports car, hoping we weren't too late. There were no cars in front of the house. There was also a drive that led to the back of the house, but I couldn't see around the back of the property. If she took a taxi, then it would make sense that she could be waiting inside for Terrance.

As I got out of the car, I could see what looked like fresh tire tracks leading around to the back. That made me really uneasy. I looked at Momma. "You wait here and call Jake. Do not get out of this car, Momma. Promise me?" I handed her my phone. "I don't have a good feeling about this. Terrance and I will go in."

"I promise. The signal is too spotty out here. I'll send a text and maybe he'll be more likely to get it." Momma punched away on the cell.

Terrance and I eased up the creaky steps. The front door was standing open just enough to see inside the front room. I couldn't see anyone in the front room so I eased it open and tiptoed in. The musty old house looked like its owners had just gone on vacation and never came home. Just as before, furniture was covered with sheets, paintings still hanging lopsided on the walls, candlesticks on the mantel. Even a pitcher and glasses sitting on an antique sideboard. I remembered the words in the letter to Sam from his father. He must have taken Sam and simply walked out, leaving everything behind that reminded him of this place.

"Judith?" I called out tentatively. When no one answered, I motioned for Terrance to search one side of the house and I took the other.

I slipped through the dining room and into the kitchen stopping dead in my tracks. Peering out from behind the kitchen island were two feet in orthopedic shoes and support hose. I forced myself to walk around the island. I'd never seen her, but I was sure it was Judith Lindsey staring up at me with cold, lifeless eyes. A puddle of blood lay around her head and a large, brass candle-stick lay innocently nearby.

Just then a noise came from the back of the house. Stifling a scream, I looked around frantically for Terrance. He was nowhere to be seen so I quietly made my way down the hall. The door to the bedroom where Momma had found the necklace was cracked open and I could hear muffled sounds.

I stepped across the threshold into the room. Then everything went black.

When I opened my eyes, my head was pounding like it was going to split wide open. I tried to move, but realized I was tied to the foot of the four-poster bed with what looked like tasseled drapery cords.

"What in the heck?" I whispered under my breath.

"No need to whisper Miss Nosy Britches." A voice came from the other corner of the room behind me. I tried to turn my head around, but it hurt too much to move it. I didn't need to, though. I recognized the syrupy sweet southern accent.

"Jeannie?" I asked in disbelief. "What on earth?"

"I had this all figured out to a tee but then you and your nosy momma just HAD to stick your noses in and mess it all up," she spat.

In my mind's eye, all the puzzle pieces started falling into place. "You killed J.R.? When we spoke that day in your office, you weren't even on my radar. I was so concerned with Terrance's alibi that it didn't occur to me that you would have had plenty of time to kill J.R. and still get to the boat in time for lunch with Terrance."

She smiled, "Yes, I followed that jerk to the church and waited in the ladies' room until I saw him walk toward the back of the church to the office. It was perfect. There was just one problem, I left my knife in the car. It must have fallen out of my pocket when I got out."

"So, you killed him with MY letter opener?"

"That was just dumb luck!" She smiled, a terrifyingly blank look in her eyes. "I dragged him right out the back door and sat him by that tree, wiped off the letter opener and threw it down next to him all while y'all were in there singing 'Leaning on the Everlasting Arms.' I knew they couldn't link that letter opener to me and it might point them to someone else. I had no idea it would be you! Bonus!"

"You did all this for Terrance didn't you? You're in love with him. So the two of you could have the business to yourselves and run it the way you wanted." I reasoned out loud. "And now poor Judith!"

"Ha! Poor Judith, poor Judith, poor Judith . . ." she kept saying in a mocking sing-song voice. "She just wouldn't come off that price. She was crazy as a loon and deserved to die!" She screamed.

"And her little nephew is gonna get the blame. It's gonna be obvious to everyone that he was just out to get his inheritance a little early."

A noise came from behind her and Jeannie spun around on her heel where Terrance stood in shock listening to her confess everything. Her tone immediately changed. Almost like there was another Jeannie in the room.

"Baby! What are you doing here? I didn't want you to be worried with all this! You are already so stressed with work. I was just gonna take care of this little problem for us!" She cooed in a lovey-dovey voice. "Now it will just have to be our little secret and we can live happily ever after!"

Terrance stood in shock.

"How did you know about the necklace?" I asked.

Psycho Jeannie was back. "As if it's any of your business. Terrance found it one day when he was out here walking the property. He put it back where he found it and then told me all about it. We researched that family and found out all about the skeletons in their pathetic family closet. We're gonna sell that lovely little bauble and use it to buy this property and finance the condo development that will make us rich!" Her eyes were wild.

She turned to Terrance, slipping in and out of two personalities as smooth as silk. "You just wait here, Honey Bun, while I decide what to do with Nancy Drew, here."

She reached behind her back and pulled a Smith & Wesson Bodyguard .380 out of her waistband. It was just like the one in my bedside table at home. *Why didn't I think to bring mine along?* I thought, mentally slapping myself. Dave had made me take that class to get certified with a handgun for my safety. I was pretty darn good at target practice if I do say so myself. Of course, it wasn't helping me at the moment. "It doesn't do any good if you don't take it with you." I could hear Dave saying. It didn't look like that was going to matter much longer.

"I think I'll just shoot you and put you in your car and push you into the lake. They will never think to look for you there." Jeannie was enjoying this way too much. She bent down to untie me from the bedpost.

"Please, Jeannie! You can't do this! It's wrong!" Terrance begged in a trembling voice. "You don't want to make this worse than it already is."

"Baby, what difference is one more going to make? We just need to get this over with and get out of here." She motioned toward the corner of the bedroom. "Go pull up the board and get the necklace while I get rid of her."

Jeannie stood over me with the gun pointed straight at my head . Terrance dove for her and grabbed her arm to pull it down. The gun went off and Terrance fell to the floor clutching his leg.

"Oh, Sweetie! Why did you have to do that? Now you're hurt!" As she bent down to see about Terrance, the door burst open.

"Drop the gun! Police!" Jake shouted.

CHAPTER 16

*M*acy and Momma were right on his heels. Macy untied me and helped me up from the dingy floor. My head pounded and my knees buckled as someone caught me before I could hit the floor again. With my spinning head, I wasn't sure who was holding me up, but the arms were strong and all I knew was that in that moment I felt safe again. And it was a good feeling. Finally steadied, I looked up into blue eyes that I immediately recognized.

"Chief Walker--- thank you, I think I'm fine now." I awkwardly pulled away and stood as tall and steady as I could.

"I want you to let the EMT's look at that whack on your head." He said as he gently reached to brush my hair away from my eyes. "And please, call me Hunt."

Jake had restrained Jeannie and handed her over to the uniformed officers that had arrived then called for an ambulance for Terrance.

"How did you know how to find us?" I asked, finally breathing easier now.

"Well for one thing, you left your Nancy Drew notepad on the kitchen table," Macy laughed. "So I called Uncle Jake."

I remembered circling the place and time on the notepad. Thank goodness for my absent minded doodling.

"By the time Macy called me and told me she thought y'all might be going to do something really stupid, Josie at the motel had called and was concerned because you left the motel in such a hurry. Then, on the way out here I started getting texts from Momma, so I called in to the station for backup," Jake explained. "I hope you see you had a lot of people that love you really worried."

I looked at all of them apologetically.

"When you didn't come right back out, I snuck around back and saw that dark blue car you thought followed you home. I peeked through the bedroom window and realized you were in real trouble. That's when I just kept texting and calling Jake, Macy, and Kelly until I got through to someone."

I hugged Momma close then I pulled away from her and looked at Jake. "Judith is dead. Jeannie confessed to killing J.R. as well."

"I know. We found her in the kitchen. I'll call Sam as soon as we get done here," Jake said. "We'll get all the details later. After you let someone look at that head, just go home and get some rest."

After checking in with an EMT and sporting a lovely bandage on the back of my head, I watched a uniformed

officer place a handcuffed Jeannie in the back of the squad
car and another EMT tending to Terrance's injuries. The
coroner's van had just arrived to transport Judith's body
to the ME's office. Chief Walker --- Hunt --- walked over
and opened the passenger's side door of my car and
helped me into the seat while Momma buckled in to drive
and Macy followed us home. I took a deep breath and said
a silent prayer of thanks for keeping us all safe through
the chaos of the last few hours.

* * *

Momma sat rocking away in the rocking chair on my
front porch as I pushed with my feet so Kelly and I could
swing higher and higher, giggling like teenagers. I swiped
my hair out of my eyes and gingerly felt the bandage still
covering the wound from Jeannie's gun. Thankfully, it
hadn't required stitches or shaving. The old chains
holding the swing squeaked with each sway. Jake stood
manning the grill while Macy threw the ball for Izzy in
the yard.

"By the way," Jake said, "the rental car company called
Pastor Dan to let him know that the church's bank bag
had been found in one of their rental cars. It still had all
the money in it. "

"That's definitely a miracle!" I exclaimed.

"Also, when I checked the security cameras from the
Quik Stop, it was Jeannie's rental car that followed you
home."

"Fat lot of good that information does me now!" I said
grinning at my baby brother.

"I just didn't want you to think I was slacking on my job."

"Never." I enjoyed giving him a hard time, but I knew Sweetwater Springs was in good hands.

As if on cue, a truck turned into the driveway and I watched in shock as Hunt Walker got out and sauntered up the sidewalk. He was carrying a jug of sweet tea and box of store-bought cookies.

I glanced over at Jake, a look of total confusion on my face and he grinned.

"I hope it's okay, I invited Chief Walker to join us. He doesn't know a lot of people in town yet."

I glared back and I heard Kelly snicker in the swing next to me. I elbowed her in the ribs.

"My momma taught me to never come to visit without bringing something to contribute to the meal," Hunt said with a grin as big as Dallas. I had to admit he looked good in his jeans, black t-shirt and cowboy boots. He smiled at me as he walked up the steps onto the porch. I got up out of the swing and took the tea and cookies from him. He smelled good, too and my heart jumped.

"It was so nice of Sam to lower the price of the property so Terrance could afford it," Momma commented, obviously oblivious to the awkwardness in the air.

"Yes, I ran into Sam at Moody's this morning and offered to buy him a cup of coffee as an apology. After all, I did suspect him of being a murderer. We sat down and he finally filled me in on the whole story of what he's been dealing with the last several months. He said that after he received the letter from his father, it had taken him months to track down Judith. She was somewhat of a recluse and was pretty much unplugged from the rest of the world. She didn't even own a cell phone. When he finally found a phone number for her, he was able to talk to her about the letter his father had left for him. He explained that all these years, he was led to believe that John's sister, Mary was his mother. She never married and since they had the same last name, no one ever questioned that he wasn't her child. She had always told him that his father was killed in a car accident when he was a baby. When his father passed away in prison, she gave him the letter that was only to be given to him after John's death. Judith wasn't completely convinced that he was who he said he was, but she had agreed to meet with him while he was in Sweetwater Springs since she was going to be here to look at the property anyway."

"Were they ever able to actually meet face to face?" Macy asked.

"No, they were scheduled to meet at the Lake House Café that night after she toured the house with Terrance. It breaks my heart that he was never able to meet his aunt face to face and that she was never able to get to know him. He's such a nice young man," I said solemnly.

"I can imagine all this new information was a horrible shock for him." Kelly said.

"He said it really hasn't sunk in yet. And on top of the shock of finding out who your real father is, he stops by to say hello to old college friends and finds out that he has a son . . . and then gets caught up in a murder investigation as the main suspect! This last week has been a roller coaster ride for him, I'm sure!"

"Did he say what his plans are going forward?" Hunt asked.

"He is obviously still in love with Linda and she with him, but they are going to take it slow. Especially for Matthew's sake, so he and Sam can get to know each other. He hopes that they will get married and raise Matthew together. He said that he could never live on the Lindsey property, so he has agreed to sell it to Terrance at a very reasonable price. At least this way, he will be able to help make something beautiful out of all this. With the money from the necklace, he will be able to buy a nice house with a bigger back yard for Matthew." I was happy for them. Especially for little Matthew who would have the chance to know his real father. One that loves him and his mommy very much.

"Speaking of real estate, I heard that Terrance has already been in touch with a resort developer and has several investors lined up for his vacation condos." Jake commented.

"Yes! And Sam also told me that Terrance has offered him the job as the lead architect to design the resort. I really think this has the potential for turning the economy of the town around. I know I may be a little biased, but I love my town and I would love for visitors to see it and love it as much as we do."

"Well, I'm liking it more and more every day." Hunt looked over at me and flashed those pearly whites and I felt something weird in my stomach. I think I must need to lay off the sugar.

"Who would ever have thought Sweetwater Springs

would become a vacation destination?" Macy exclaimed as she tossed the ball and Izzy went racing after it.

I noticed the slightest hint of a worried frown come across Jake's face. "I'm not looking forward to all the fires I'm gonna have to put out over the next few months with that project. There are several powerful people that are up in arms about it." Hunt nodded in agreement.

"I'm just thanking the good Lord for a peaceful town again and praying for it to stay that way for awhile." Momma said.

Macy's phone was lying on the top porch step as it vibrated an incoming call. I glanced down and saw that it was Tony, her friend from school. She ran over, grabbed it up and slid her finger across to answer the call.

"Hey!" I heard her say, just catching bits and pieces of the one-sided conversation. "Great! What time will you get here?" followed by another pause . . . "See you then! . . . You too! . . . Bye."

I caught her eye and smiled. "Someone coming for a visit?"

"He'll be here tomorrow afternoon, by the time we get home from church! I can't wait for you all to meet him," she said beaming. I could tell this was not just any friend.

I was still a little overwhelmed with everything that had happened in the last few days.

I looked at Momma rocking on the porch, whistling a little hymn to herself; at Kelly swinging away beside me and laughing; at Jake and Hunt, flipping the steaks and Macy playing with Izzy in the yard. Knowing I would have my girl living back in town near me made me so happy. I was excited about her future with the bakery and coffee shop and helping her get it up and running. I was surrounded by people I loved. Deep down, I felt the anticipation of something new on the horizon and I was reminded of one of my favorite verses in the Bible.

"And we know that all things work together for good to those who love God, to those who are the called according to His purpose." Romans 8:28

He truly had made good things come from the evil intentions of bad people.

I smiled and breathed a prayer of thanks for all my blessings and that I truly was back home.

RECIPES

GLORY'S HODGE PODGE SOUP

Skill Level: Easy Peasy

Ingredients:

3-4 lbs ground beef, browned & drained

½ small onion (whole onion if you like more)

3 cans Minestrone soup (I like Progresso)

2 cans Rotel tomatoes (I use mild, but you can use original or hot)

2 T chili powder

1 can water

Worcestershire sauce to taste

Garlic powder to taste

Instructions:

Sauté onions in butter or olive oil in bottom of large pot.

Add ground beef and brown. Drain or spoon out excess grease.

Add remaining ingredients and simmer one hour over med-low heat.

Stir frequently to prevent scorching/sticking.

Serve with crackers (we like oyster crackers)

MOMMA'S MEXICAN CORNBREAD

Skill Level: Easy

Ingredients:
    1 ½ cups cornmeal
    ½ teaspoon salt
    1 med. onion
    ½ cup grated cheddar cheese
    1 cup cream corn
    ¼ cup milk
    ½ cup oil
    2 eggs
    Diced jalapeño peppers (to taste)

Instructions:
    Preheat oven to 375⁰
    Combine all ingredients and mix thoroughly.
    Pour into greased muffin tins or medium iron skillet.
    Bake for 20-30 minutes in skillet (or until pick inserted in center comes out clean)
    Bake for 14-16 minutes for standard muffins.
    Makes about 1 dozen muffins or a medium iron skillet of cornbread.

MACY'S FRENCH MACARONS

Skill Level: Medium/Advanced

Ingredients:

¾ Cup powdered sugar

¾ Cup almond flour

2 Large egg whites (at room temp)

½ Cup granulated sugar

Food coloring if desired (added to egg whites)

Instructions:

Preheat oven to 300⁰

Line 2-3 baking sheets with parchment.

Sift together almond flour and powdered sugar. Set aside.

Beat egg whites in mixer. (add coloring if desired)

When foamy, add granulated sugar (gradually)

Continue to beat until stiff.

Fold egg whites into almond/powdered sugar dry mixture until well combined and has a lava-like consistency.

Transfer to piping bag.

Pipe vertically onto parchment forming desired size round cookie shapes. Leave ½ inch gap between cookies. Let them sit to form "skin". Approx.. 45 minutes.

Bake 15 minutes. Careful not to overcook.

Let cool on sheet before transferring to wire cooling rack.

Fill with desired filling and enjoy.

Makes about 40 cookies (20 filled macarons)

ABOUT THE AUTHOR

S.C. Merritt is a Cozy Mystery author whose stories
feature southern female sleuths, plots with a twist and a
little sprinkle of romance. The Sweetwater Springs
Southern Mystery Series is set in a small Alabama town
full of quirky characters, delicious restaurants and lots of
murder.
Yummy recipes are included in each book!
When not writing, she is traveling, watching classic
movies and tv shows or collecting flamingos.
She lives in Mississippi with her husband and miniature
Schnauzer, Izzy and dreams of living in a tropical locale
someday.

You can find out all about new releases and sign up for
her monthly CozyLetter at: www.scmerritt.com
And don't forget to follow her on the following:

facebook.com/scmerrittwrites

amazon.com/author/scmerritt

bookbub.com/authors/s-c-merritt

goodreads.com/19874419.S_C_Merritt

instagram.com/scmerrittauthor

pinterest.com/scmerrittwrites

OTHER BOOKS BY S.C. MERRITT

<u>Sweetwater Springs Southern Mysteries</u>

Potluck and Pandemonium

Lakefronts and Larceny (coming March 2020)

Moonshine and Murder (coming Summer 2020)

LAKEFRONTS AND LARCENY
(COMING MARCH 2020)

"Girl, we look good!" I laughingly commented as I leaned across the glass topped bakery display case and spread out the latest copy of the Sweetwater Herald. The photo splashed across the front page showed Macy, grinning from ear to ear, her boyfriend, Antonio Castellini, and me, a very proud mom. Standing alongside us were several members of the Sweetwater Springs Chamber of Commerce looking on as the Mayor used a gigantic pair of scissors to cut the ribbon, symbolizing the Grand Opening of Macy's On Main, Hometown Bakery and Beanery. After months of tearing out wood paneling, refinishing original hardwood floors, installing a state-of-the-art commercial baking kitchen and a plethora of cappuccino, espresso and coffee appliances, her dream had become a reality. I was so proud of my girl that I could bust wide open.

Macy had just brought out a warm pan of from-scratch, blueberry biscuits and started arranging them on a tray for the morning rush. "We look awesome except for that goofy grin on my face!" she commented as she drizzled the warm sugar glaze over the biscuits. "Why do I have to show every tooth in my mouth?"

"I think it's a great picture," I said as I took a bite of the warm biscuit and groaned in delight. "And how cool is it that soon there'll be a picture of Tony's ribbon cutting for Tavolo? I think the grand opening of two new eateries in Sweetwater Springs in the same month must be the biggest thing to happen here since the county seceded from the state during the Civil War," I said, referring to the history that was our town and county's claim to fame. When the State of Alabama seceded from the Union, our county was so opposed to the Confederacy, it seceded from the state. There was even a big statue of a half Confederate, half Union soldier in the center of town to commemorate the event.

"I'm so excited for both of us. A little scared, but excited." Macy confided. "He's been so good to help me even with his own place opening in a couple of weeks."

Macy's former chef instructor, turned boyfriend, had volunteered to come over from Mississippi back in May and help her with her bakery design and menu planning. Over the last few months, not only had he fallen in love with the town, but it seems he had fallen in love with Macy. As they worked together on her bakery and coffee shop plans, he got the idea to purchase the storefront next door and open an Italian restaurant. From the little bit of information I could drag out of Macy, this wasn't the first time he had owned his own place. Tony had been co-owner in a restaurant somewhere up north several years ago but made the decision to leave the restaurant business to teach culinary school. I guess he was ready to give it another shot. He was quite a bit older than Macy, so it took me awhile to get used to the idea that he's closer to my age than to hers, but it didn't take me long to see what she saw in him. He had such a kind and generous heart. It was easy to see that he loved and believed in Macy. They supported each other in their new business ventures, and it was going to be fun to see where their relationship went.

I walked over to the coffee area and poured myself a large iced coffee to go. "I hate to leave you, but I need to head on in to work. Nana should be here any minute to help you out."

"I just put the last of the dark chocolate pound cakes in to bake. Once she gets here, she can start mixing up the cranberry pecan crisps and I'll work out front."

The bakery had only been open a couple of weeks and we knew Macy couldn't afford to pay anyone to help just yet, so Momma and I were tag teaming. She worked on Monday and Wednesday, the days I worked in the office at Sweetwater Springs Baptist Church, and I planned to work with Macy on the other days. From the conversations I'd had with Momma, she seemed to be a little overwhelmed. "How is she doing with her barista lessons?" I asked as I straightened tables and chairs across the room.

"Pretty good. I don't think she expected it to be as complicated as it is, but she's actually catching on pretty quickly," Macy answered as she flipped the switch on both coffeemakers.

"I can sympathize with her. Some of these machines

are complicated and it seems that these days it's become more of an art form!" I laughed.

The bell over the door jingled and Momma flipped the sign on the door to OPEN as she came breezing in. "Mornin' Macy! Mornin' Glory!" Momma beamed. Everyone got such a kick out of greeting me that way, including Momma.

"Well, you sound chipper on this Monday morning!" I laughed.

"Good morning, Nana. Do you mind working on some cookies in the kitchen this morning?"

"I'll do whatever helps you the most." Momma said tying an apron around her waist and heading through the swinging door with a smile of complete relief. Momma was well-known for being one of the best cooks in town. The cooking gene skipped a generation with me, but I was glad Macy got it.

The door jingled again, as Megan Lester and a lady I didn't recognize, came in dressed to the nines and started browsing the pastry selection in the display case. "Good morning ladies! What can I get for you this morning?" Macy chirped. "The blueberry biscuits are to die for, if I do say so myself."

"I'll take one of those and a skinny vanilla latte," Megan responded.

Megan was the president of our local Ladies' Club and southern to the core. My Granny would say that she always "put on the dog", which meant she acted a little uppity. When I first met Megan, I thought the same thing, but the more I'd gotten to know her, the more I think she's just a true southern belle. She has a kind heart and had never been anything but nice to me and she and the other ladies had welcomed me into the Ladies' Club with open arms. Maybe they saw me as new blood and it probably helped that I had a problem saying 'no' and usually regretted it later. I had gotten in over my head on several occasions, one of which I was in the middle of now.

"I think I'll go with the chocolate croissant and a cup of whatever your boldest roast coffee is this morning," Megan's friend said as they took a seat at one of the bistro tables on the other side of the room.

Even standing at the counter several feet away, I could still hear bits and pieces of their conversation. The lady with Megan was clearly adamant about something and Megan kept nodding her head like she was agreeing with her. I heard the word condo and my radar immediately went on full alert. Construction on a group of resort condominiums called Pine Bluffs was just getting underway out on Smith Lake. Although many people in town were excited about the potential it had to bring in the tourist trade, there was a pocket of citizens who were adamantly against it. These were mostly made up of lake-front landowners whose property was near the resort.

Macy arranged the blueberry biscuit and chocolate croissant on cute mismatched, vintage dessert plates and placed them on a serving tray on the counter along with their coffee orders. I took the opportunity to get a little closer to the conversation and delivered the delicious goodies myself.

"I don't know about you and Chris, but Jeff and I are

not going to stand for it," the other lady was saying. "Our property values have already taken a hit and they've barely broken ground."

Megan nodded. "Believe me, Chris feels the same way. We need to do *whatevah* it takes to get this project stopped before it goes any *fuh-tha*," Megan continued in her Scarlett O'Hara southern drawl. "Don't you worry your sweet little head. I have a feeling we won't have that little problem much *longa, dah-ling*."

"Here you go, ladies. Best breakfast in town!" I smiled as I placed the plates in front of them along with their coffees.

"This smells just divine!" Megan exclaimed. "Macy is as sweet as tea and this place is just heavenly. I know it's gonna be a glorious success."

"Thanks, Megan. I'm pretty proud of her," I smiled and turned to the other lady as she took her first bite of the croissant and groaned in delight. "I don't think we've met. My name is Glory Harper. I'm Macy's mom. I'm in the Ladies' Club with Megan."

"Oh, Glory, I do apologize! I thought you had met Cindy," Megan said placing her hand daintily on the other lady's arm. "This is Cindy Newsome. She is in the Ladies' Club with us. She and her husband, Jeff, own Hearth and Home Furniture."

"Nice to meet you, Glory. Since summer is our slowest time for sales, we use that time to travel to various trade shows and furniture markets to get ready for the fall which is our busiest time of year. I have had to miss the last few meetings. I hate missing out on all the fun, but business comes before anything else at our house," Cindy smiled.

"I didn't mean to eavesdrop," I said with my fingers crossed behind my back, "but I couldn't help overhearing your conversation about the condo project. I know Megan's position on it, but I take it that you and your husband are opposed to it also?"

I knew Megan and Chris Lester were one hundred percent against the project. They lived on the *upper* end of the lake and that's where the condos were being built. Commercial buildings like the boat docks, bait store, jet ski rentals, Lakeside Motel and Lake House Café were all much further down the shoreline. A few months ago, Megan had commented to me that Terrance Wolfe had better "watch his back" if he tried to move forward with the project.

"Yes. We live next to Megan and Chris on the Upper End and are just as concerned as everyone else that the commercial rentals will destroy our property values. And let's not forget the ambiance on the Upper End that we paid a pretty penny to acquire." Cindy lifted her coffee cup to take a drink with her pinky finger stuck out a mile.

"I see. I can understand your concerns, but don't you feel like the beauty of our lake is something that everyone should be able to enjoy? God's beauty in nature really belongs to everyone, right? Hopefully, this will boost the economy of our town and as a result your furniture business will grow."

"Maybe," Cindy frowned and shrugged as she took another sip of her coffee.

"Well, ladies, I hope you have a wonderful day. I need

to get moving if I'm going to make it to the church office on time." I returned the serving tray to Macy at the counter and told her I'd see her tonight and headed to work.

GET LAKEFRONTS AND LARCENY NOW!

Made in the USA
Coppell, TX
21 November 2020

41841246R00111